# PERIHELION

TAMI VELDURA

OLDEWOLFF ALTERNASCENTS

Ramona, California

Oldewolff Alternascents, an imprint of Oldewolff Prints
326 Oak St
Ramona, California 92065

Publisher's Note: This is a work of fiction. Names, characters, places, and incidents are a product of the author's imagination. Locales and public names are sometimes used for atmospheric purposes. Any resemblance to actual people, living or dead, or to businesses, companies, events, institutions, or locales is completely coincidental.

Book Layout ©2013 BookDesignTemplates.com & wrangled by OWEnt. Cover Design by Tami Veldura, protected under a creative commons At-tribution, Non Commercial, No Derivatives license. Cover art ©2015 by Max Bedulenko, all rights reserved, used with permission. Free commercial fonts by Font Squirrel. Title Font: GreatLakesNF.

Ordering Information:
Quantity sales. Special discounts are available on quantity purchases by corporations, associations, and others. For details, contact the "Special Sales Department" at the address above.

PERIHELION/ Tami Veldura -- 1st ed.
ISBN 978-1-941319-11-6

## M/M GOODREADS GROUP

This story was written as a part of the M/M Romance Group's "Love's Landscapes" event. Group members were asked to write a story prompt inspired by a photo of their choice. Authors of the group selected a photo and prompt that spoke to them and wrote a short story.

## PHOTO DESCRIPTION:

A naked man rises from a tank of glowing blue liquid. Ports line his neck and ribs with cords extending from them, plugged into something unseen (and out of the picture). His skin is embedded with glowing circuits, and his shaved head bows forward. Mist floats around him as electric currents or lightning strikes illuminate the background.

**DEAR AUTHOR,**

I woke up to the sight of him coming out of a healing tank. I realized that I knew nothing but that this man was important to me. Please have this be in the middle of the story. I want to know what caused my amnesia, what we were before the amnesia, and what happened after this.

I think this will be sci-fi—my only requirements are no tentacles, and I want a HFN or HEA. If we are of different species or races, it does not matter. Please tell me my story.

Sincerely,
Roger

*If you wish
to make an apple pie
from scratch,*

*you must first
invent the universe.*

**—CARL SAGAN**

## KATO: *QUEENSHIP SELVANS*

KATO FINGERED the overstarched cuff of his dress blues. The pins on his left breast glinted under the light, and he twitched his shoulders back. Ceren flicked his elbow from her place behind him, and he corrected his hands. Down at his hips, thumbs in line with the seam. He inched his right boot further into the tie-down keeping him in place. He took a deep breath. The women in line to either side of him did the same.

"Relax," Ceren whispered.

Kato shifted to one side and shot her a brief, narrow eye roll. "Easy for—"

First Commander Reza Ahmadi floated onto the bridge—her boots tapped like a countdown on the composite floor as she slid them into tie-downs. Everyone in the room stiffened to attention. Kato bit his tongue. The first commander said nothing. She faced the assembled lines of soldiers but stared past them at the generated images and display screens of the bridge. Kato resisted the urge to look behind him.

Ceren flicked his elbow again, and he tried to do as she bid. He unclenched his jaw and let his breath out in a slow stream. He couldn't imagine how she managed to be so cavalier. She was on the shortlist for pilot, but he was the one in knots over a possible bridge assistant position. If his record was strong enough. If his grandmother's name held enough sway. If his mother's name didn't tarnish his entire reputation.

The first commander held her hands behind her back and turned her attention from one screen to another. "Final egress check?"

From behind Kato, a woman seated and strapped at a terminal said, "In progress. Personnel are counted. All outer doors are sealed and locked." A pause. Then, "Communication with Lempo remains clear. We are ready for egress on your mark, First Commander."

The first commander spent another moment assessing information on the screens, and her delay crawled up Kato's spine. In seconds their ship would push off into free space and Lempo's daughter would come to life. He heard Ceren take a quick breath and hold it. And he guessed at her reaction—the looming possibility of finally attaining a pilot's mantle perhaps setting her nerves on fire. He knew the feeling.

"Undock and burn rear thrusters at ten percent for five seconds," the first commander said.

Located at the ship's fore, Kato was too distant to hear the coupling disengage. The ship's mass was so great that the powerful thruster burn was reduced to a mild hum. Behind Kato the woman said, "All personnel, prepare for queenship awakening." Her voice spread through the room and every corridor on the ship.

Then the bridge went black. Kato jumped. Soldiers around him stifled their surprise and maintained formation. The hum of ventilation fans wound to a stop.

Kato saw lights blink back on down the hall connecting the bridge to the rest of the ship. The main spine. The lights shimmered forward, a wave of power that engulfed the bridge and rippled down the body of the ship. Kato swore the entire thing shuddered. Then, an androgynous voice came from every direction at once.

*I am Selvans.*

The first commander smiled. "Good morning, Selvans. I am First Commander Reza Ahmadi. Please perform a full self-diagnostic."

Lights blinked in sequence, and a man behind Kato spoke quietly at a terminal.

The ship said: *I am fully functional and self-aware.*

The woman behind Kato said, "Confirmed, First Commander. Lempo has given us a green light."

"Very good. Selvans, are you prepared to select your pilot?"

Selvans replied: *Yes, First Commander.*

Kato heard Ceren let out all her breath. He tucked his right hand behind his thigh and crossed his fingers, knowing she'd see it.

"Do so now."

A sense of black space bloomed in the back of Kato's mind. He imagined Ceren feeling the ship, and he knew her breath was coming in short, anticipatory bursts. He felt her chest flutter. The fluid-like gas they all breathed circled around the bridge, around the entire ship—a space-traveling ocean of life-forms. A complete biome.

Kato sensed Selvans drifting away from Lempo. With distance, the mother queenship resolved into a massive sphere. Drones swarmed the surface, shuttling people and supplies down to Earth or beyond. His sense of scale abruptly shifted. Kato struggled to grasp an understanding of the entire interstellar neighborhood made up of a dozen or so of their closest stars.

His mind tried to stretch further, and he cried out. He squeezed his eyes shut and dug his fingers into his curly hair. He felt a hand grab a loop on his belt and tug him down. Then hands on his shoulders, fingers grabbing his.

Kato's mind zipped down to local space and then snapped back into his own head. He opened his eyes with a gasp of relief. His arms fell slack. Ceren's cool thumbs stroked the top of his brow, and Kato realized she was speaking. Her voice sounded far away for a moment. Then that snapped back into place, too.

"—ust breathe Kato. You're going to be fine. Relax, and let her in. She's not going to hurt you."

Kato coughed. "Fuck me..."

Ceren barked a laugh and held his head between her palms. "You back with us?"

"Yeah..." Except the lingering understanding of space wouldn't leave the edges of his awareness. "Yeah, I'm OK."

"Pilot Kato Ozark," the first commander said. "Welcome aboard."

Kato reached for a tie-down overhead, and Ceren helped turn him around. The first commander held a transparent slate that glowed with text. His entire file, no doubt. He monkeyed forward until he could float in front of her, aware that drifting into her would not make a good impression.

"Says here your grandmother pilots Queen Lempo."

"Yes, sir." Kato tried to stay at attention. Some sense of knowing teased him, tempted him to look around the ship without even moving.

"I also see your mother—"

"Sir, I have no affiliation with my mother. They wouldn't have ever let me on the ship."

The first commander lowered her slate and pursed her lips. "Quite." She offered her hand. "Then let me be the first to congratulate you."

Kato pushed himself down another few inches to grasp her hand. He fell into the first commander's head. Forty-seven, six foot even, cancer survivor, genetic risk for high blood pressure—he tried to wrench his hand out of her grip and failed—previous service record aboard Lempo not without its blemishes but generally positive. However her assignment here was a case of failing upward—a fact she wasn't proud of in the slightest. Kato sensed an immense respect and loyalty for Pilot Farai. *Kato.* He couldn't stop the flow of information. Kato dove into Reza Ahmadi's years aboard Lempo. In moments, he relived every success and failure; he retained those memories as if they were his. He knew her struggle with—*KATO!*

He jerked back into himself. His left hand drifted off the ceiling. His right hand still clasped Reza's. He met her golden eyes, flecked like amber, and licked his lips. What did he do now? He'd never understood anyone at such an intimate level, closer than twins. It was an invasion he knew Reza would give almost anything to take back.

"I'm s—" He swallowed his words at the slight tightening of her mouth. Her eyes hardened a fraction further. Details he wouldn't have noticed without knowing her as he just did. He straightened his shoulders. "Thank you." For the congratulations. For the gift of her history, even though it wasn't her choice. "I'll do my best."

"I know."

And Kato wondered if the knowing hadn't gone both ways. How much of him had Reza seen while he drowned in her head?

She released his hand, and Kato's attention immediately shifted down the hall. No one was there, but he was drawn to it, regardless. He tried to redirect his attention to the first commander and found himself struggling.

"Go. No doubt Selvans has much to show you."

"...What?"

Ceren laughed. Kato grabbed a handhold to turn around. The hand-selected thirty stared back at him. "You nerd," Ceren teased with a smile. "She chose you. You're the damn pilot."

And the obviousness of it struck him like a blow to the face. He couldn't get enough air. He wanted to grab Ceren. Maybe hug her. He needed something to stabilize him. He yearned across the gap. *I'm not prepared for this; I'm supposed to be a bridge assistant.*

Ceren laughed again as if she'd heard him. Then the need to move pressed in on him, and Kato swung up to the ceiling. He pulled himself into the hall by the tie-downs, Selvans' desires guiding him.

## Mas'ud: *Queenship Selvans*

Mas'ud Tavana scrolled through a new design on the wall slate. He zoomed out and rotated the image of the queenship to frown at the back end. Angled sprouts of crystal-like structure tapered down to the single massive engine. The design was functional but he couldn't say it was effective. Not if they were going into contested space. "How many drones do we have on board?"

He didn't have rebuild authority, but as first engineer it was his duty to provide improvement suggestions to the pilot. Whoever that would be. If they were flying out to the fringe of the spiral arm they needed to deploy their fighters faster than anyone else. Faster than Dhar.

"Close to seven thousand," Amala said. She pressed the edge of her slate against his wall screen and swiped a box of numbers over. Her headscarf drifted around her shoulders. "About a hundred of them are collection-class."

Mas'ud sucked his teeth. Amala grabbed a tie-down on the wall to stay in place. "You don't like it."

"I do like it. That's the problem." Mas'ud spun the design. "But there isn't enough surface area to release seven thousand drones and—how many kings? Doesn't matter. It'll take us five minutes to deploy everyone."

His second turned down one side of her mouth. "You really think we're headed into the front lines? Pru is at the edge of the arm. I'm not even sure it's Ozark-controlled."

A new engineer said, "We've undocked."

Mas'ud shrank the design and, with a gesture, threw it off his screen. "I think that Pilot Farai wouldn't send her brand-new queen into the farthest reach of her territory for a checkup on some maybe-loyal colony. So I'm—"

The intercom said: *All personnel—Prepare for queenship awakening.*

"Everyone grab a tie-down," Mas'ud said. He reached for one overhead.

The power cut out. Engineering went black, and someone whispered *oh, shit.* Mas'ud tried not to think about their relatively small boat floating in the vast nothing without any defense or ability to correct course. Then the lights surged back on, and everyone let out a tense breath.

*I am Selvans.*

"All right, folks. The bridge is going to be occupied all day with getting our new pilot sorted out, so here's what I want: Scrap the current model. Draw up something from scratch or take inspiration from something bizarre—"

"Like what?"

"Don't care. Shark teeth if that makes you warm and fuzzy. Hey"—Mas'ud pointed to the new engineer— "what's your name?"

"Ismet Deniz, sir."

Mas'ud waved at the title. "Find us some peppy music. Orchestral. I want everyone trying this out. Prioritize getting every drone and king into open space in as little time as possible. Ignore every functional restriction. Uncheck all the boxes and play with the design. We can make it work later."

Amala pushed away from the wall. "You, too, Zola."

A woman with a dark complexion and bright pale eyes looked up. "Really?"

"You're on a co-op, here? You know the program?" Mas'ud asked.

"Yes, sir."

"Good, you won't have any bad habits. Give me something I've never seen before."

She grinned at him. "Yes, sir!"

Mas'ud rolled his eyes at the title, but Amala caught the look, and he didn't say anything. She was still trying to convince him he deserved it. The position, he craved—but the title could vent with their flotsam for all he cared.

Mas'ud slid his hand on the ceiling to turn himself and felt a shock of longing/connection/incompleteness. He whipped his head around in the direction of the bridge—specifically, to the exact location he somehow knew the pilot's cockpit to be. From here all he could see was the upper corner of Engineering, but he felt the hollow space like an ache in his head. He was at an utter loss to explain it.

"Mas'ud?" Amala sounded like that wasn't the first time she'd called his name.

He dragged his eyes down to her but couldn't bring himself to pull his fingers from the ceiling. He noticed a deep crease of concern between her eyes. "I'm fine," he said too quickly. Her crease deepened, and she straightened up from the screen. Mas'ud yanked his fingertips from the ceiling—tearing/loss—and insisted, "It's nothing."

But a heavy impact of longing crashed between his eyes, and he pressed the heel of his hand to his forehead. "Wow."

Amala pushed herself to him and grabbed his arm. He fell into her emotions, swept up in her concern and the love of an old friend. It was warm. Like hot tea in front of a fire. He wanted to wrap himself up in it and never let go, so he did. He felt her surprise and dismissed it. He was safe here.

But Amala's intense confusion eventually drove him to reach out further. He touched Ismet's discomfort and Zola's hesitation. He could feel every one of his engineers. Mas'ud pushed his mind outward, and like an expanding bubble, he brushed the mind of each person in the ship. He drifted even further outward to greet Queen Lempo. Her pilot, Farai, maintained a wall between them, and the sudden blockage pushed Mas'ud back into awareness. She extended a mental handshake. Mas'ud clumsily met it. He couldn't drift and communicate at the same time, though, and his awareness pulled back, down to Engineering. Then to Amala.

Then he was alone in his head once more.

Amala stared at him, her eyes too-wide around the corners. She held the edges of her headscarf in one fist. While Mas'ud vibrated with new energy, Amala gripped his arm with fear. She whispered, "What the fuck was that?"

Mas'ud reached up to the ceiling again and lightly touched just his fingertips. Incomplete/yearning. The queenship had carried him along—Mas'ud had no doubt—and now she needed him for something. He wasn't about to refuse her. "I need to go."

"Like hell you do."

Mas'ud looked down at Amala and then around at Engineering and realized he was the center of attention. He cleared his throat and pulled his hand back down.

Zola picked up a small phone. "I'm going to call a doc—"

Even without the connection, Mas'ud felt Selvans calling to him. "Not necessary." Mas'ud grabbed Amala's shoulders and hated how she flinched. "Get started on the new design to deploy our soldiers faster. I'll be back." He pushed toward the doorway and caught himself at the threshold. "I want to see something from each of you before lunch. Get crazy."

He left Amala drifting in the center of the room, equal parts afraid and concerned. He could feel her tangle of emotion even as he launched himself down the narrow hall. He trailed his fingertips against the composite wall to feel Selvans' thoughts more clearly. She was thrilled he was on his way. Mas'ud couldn't imagine what she needed him for, but no one stopped him.

He knew every corridor of the queenship from models and prints, but actually moving toward the heart of the ship was an intense experience. The closer he got, the stronger Selvans' need grew, and Mas'ud kicked off a wall with both legs to gain speed. Decidedly not allowed under any Ozark regulation.

Mas'ud's heart raced. He clenched his fists to keep his fingers from shaking, so the instability moved to his arms and shoulders instead. He shot toward a wall, and at the last moment it irised open before him. He knew it would. Selvans needed him. The ship pulsed around him. Or maybe Mas'ud pulsed inside the ship. He felt people moving around him, going about the duties of preparing a new queenship for her maiden voyage. He grabbed a tie-down and swung feet first around a corner, angling himself up close to the ceiling to avoid a woman he/Selvans knew was there.

A guard floated at the end of the hall. He yanked himself to the side in the face of Mas'ud's momentum. When the door didn't iris open, Mas'ud slammed against the wall and clung to a tie-down. He pressed his palms and cheek to the edge of the door where metal met crystal composite. Selvans' elation surged through him. "I'm here, I'm almost there. Hold on."

The guard stammered at Mas'ud, "Ma'am, I need you to back up."

Mas'ud twitched at the misgender, but Selvans' intensity overruled his discomfort. "Open the door, Selvans."

"Ma'am—" The guard tried to insist.

The door irised open. Mas'ud yanked a tie-down and the door snapped shut behind him, cutting off whatever the guard was going to say. He drifted through a short receiving space where metals gave way to entirely composite crystal. A membrane across the entry, like muscle, pulled back, and Mas'ud entered the cockpit itself. He was not alone.

The pilot was handsome— tall, with tightly curled black hair and a wide mouth. He was staring into nothing, and Mas'ud assumed Selvans' intense presence had taken hold. It gave Mas'ud a moment to admire the hard angles of military muscle under the man's deep black skin. The short sleeves of his dress blues exposed the strength in his arms.

Selvans urged Mas'ud closer.

## JAI LI: *DHAR UNIVERSITY*

JAI LI TUGGED her gray suit jacket down even though it was already in place. She wore a small black travel backpack. Even her earrings were unaffiliated silver. She waited patiently in the security line, her family-neutral ID and boarding pass in one hand. She'd stripped her nails of color just last night. Jai Li reminded herself to relax. She couldn't afford to give any one of the Dhar security guards a reason to pay her any mind at all.

She floated forward and presented her ID and pass for inspection. The Tsui woman glanced up at her and negligently gestured at the scanner. Jai Li buckled her bag to the unit. A quick blue light blinked. All the woman would find was a change of clothes and a file-folder. Jai Li accepted her ID and pass. She boarded the Tsui drone.

Their ship took almost an hour to fill. This model sported a swollen belly four levels deep and nearly three hundred rows long. Jai Li entered at the second level in the middle of the craft. She found her spot only two rows away in the center aisle. The rows were barely wide enough for her to slide in sideways. She buckled her bag to the floor below her feet and cinched the net tight. Jai Li pushed against the row in front of her to back up into her space. She strapped in: a shoulder harness and waist buckle that left her feet dangling. Below her were loops to secure her feet, but she didn't feel the need.

People packed in tight, and the cramped space wasn't comfortable, but it wouldn't last long. Jai Li held onto the chest harness and closed her eyes.

It took longer for the drone to check their pressure seal and disengage from the Dhar-controlled space station than the actual act of warping from Alpha Centauri-C to Earth. The drone hummed, stretched, and was suddenly there, maneuvering in to dock at Queenship Lempo. A third of the Tsui drone passengers disembarked. Jai Li waited. It took another half hour to refill. Then they pulled away from Queenship Lempo and began the hour-long flight down to the surface.

The drone flew through the sky, and the transition from floating to falling was seriously disconcerting. Two seats away, someone vomited into a bag. Jai Li breathed carefully through her nose and kept her eyes closed. She'd never heard anything so loud as a transport drone landing planet-side.

Her entire row clicked and began to descend. As people's feet met the floor, the individual units paused. Jai Li's was the last to stop. She held onto the row in front of her and unbuckled one-handed. Gravity was not something she entirely trusted. She'd practiced weighted walking in a centrifugal ring, but the telltale sensation of spin was entirely missing from this experience. It took much longer for the people on board to disembark, and Jai Li was thankful to discover hand-holds and rails throughout the port.

They lead her straight to a taxi. At least this was familiar. "Dhar University, please. The north gate."

As they pulled away, the spaceport's roofline faded behind them and Jai Li gripped the taxi's door handle with white knuckles. The open sky was a wash of light blue in every possible direction. She squeezed her eyes shut and took several calming breaths. The taxi zipped through traffic.

She peeked as their speed slowed, and the enclosed feeling imposed by tall skyscrapers helped her calm down. Her brain persistently suggested everything was stuck to a ceiling and without a floor—that they would simply drop into open space. Jai Li found the inefficient nature of so many vehicles on a single plane to be almost comical, but if the alternative were falling into the sky, she'd take it.

The taxi pulled up to a guardhouse at the north gate and the driver rolled down his window. Jai Li shouted and then slapped her hand over her mouth. The driver gave her a bored look. Jai Li tried to settle her panicked heart. There was air everywhere. Outside. Inside. She was just fine. It made no sense at all.

The university guard asked for her ID. She pulled it out of her bag with shaking hands. The window didn't hiss with decompression when she rolled it down, and the lack of sound was more disconcerting than anything so far. She handed her ID to the guard and laced her fingers together tightly. He grunted and handed it back. The taxi moved forward smoothly. Jai Li squeezed her eyes shut and wished she were back in space. On a drone, on a station, on a mining asteroid—it didn't matter. At least the rules made sense there.

The taxi stopped. "Where to?"

Jai Li realized they had paused at an intersection. She dug through her bag, thankful for something to focus on. In her folder she found the room number. "Building A-three, please."

"Entrance is underground," he said and turned the wheel.

Jai Li didn't understand why that mattered until the taxi pulled into the tunnel. As soon as the building covered them her nerves settled considerably. She let out a deep breath and rubbed her face. "Thank god. What do I owe you?"

"Thirty-five, ma'am." He patted the slate built into the back of his seat.

She pressed her ID to the surface. It blinked blue and displayed her route and fare. She changed the charge to sixty and thanked the driver on her way out. In the lobby she took a moment for herself. She tugged her suit jacket down and organized her file folder. The mirror claimed she looked far more composed than she felt. At the elevator she pressed her ID to the slate until it blinked white and let her on board. She scanned her ID again on the inside, and the machine lifted her quickly to the top of the building. Jai Li grabbed the handrail in surprise.

The doors slid open. A man sat at a long desk that stretched the length of the short hall. She walked to him with one hand on the edge of the desk, back to feeling insecure in her footing. She offered her ID. "Jai Li, here, to see Nicolau Dhar, please."

The man scanned her ID yet again and typed something onto his slate. Then he slid the card into a tray on his desk. "You can go on in."

At the end of the hall, a door slid to the side. Jai Li resisted the urge to ask for her ID back. She nodded her thanks and squared her shoulders. She took a steadying breath and walked through the door. Nicolau's office was more window than walls, but the near-invisible seams between glass panes was a distortion she was familiar with. Jai Li walked up to the overlong desk, folder in one hand.

To her surprise, Nicolau stood to greet her. He was tall, over six feet at least, and his smile came easily. "Jai Li, thank you for coming all this way."

She shook his hand and then placed her folder at the edge of his desk. "It's my belief that queenship sentience is passed down to new queens similar to cloning offspring in single-sex animals."

Nicolau pet the front of his suit as he sat down. "It's in their DNA?"

Jai Li toggled one hand. "That is a passable analogy. More to the point, every queen is related in this way, cloned of the queen that birthed it, with all the knowledge that came before."

Nicolau leaned forward. "Genetic memory?"

"In effect."

"Then they know where Gaia is. They know what happened to her."

Jai Li shook her head. "We didn't start tracking family trees until only a thousand years ago. We don't know which queens are from which of Gaia's children. If they're all descended from the first queen, we can only know for sure up to that point in Gaia's history—" She waved her hand. "This isn't why you called me here. The program is complete. I've based the AI off of Queen Qu Yuan and Queen Demeter."

"In there?" Nicolau nodded to her folder.

"No, it's on my ID."

Nicolau thumbed an icon on his screen. "Bring me Jai Li's ID card, please."

A breath later, the secretary walked in, card in hand. Nicolau pressed it against the large slate and dragged the only file inside onto his display. The secretary left.

"That is the only copy," Jai Li said.

Nicolau nodded. When the transfer completed he dropped her card into a slot on his desk. Something that sounded surprisingly mechanical ground it to pieces then lasered what remained.

Jai Li took a breath. "It passes all the tests we know how to run."

"You have reservations?"

She chose her words carefully. "I... lack a complete understanding of the queen birth... Growth? Process. Pilots are understandably hesitant to share any information, and the queens, themselves..." She waved her hand. "Simulation can't possibly re-create both human mind and queen mind. It will work better than any king you have in the air, but I can't promise the mesh will work or that other queens will be willing to interact with it. They'll know it's artificial.

"Sir, I know you're building an independent queen. No one knows this AI better than me. Let me pilot the first tests." Jai Li stilled her hands on her folder.

Nicolau looked at her. "We haven't settled on a candidate, yet. Are you willing to go through vetting?"

"Of course."

He nodded. "I can't give you any preference. You either pass or you don't."

"I understand." She finally pushed the folder toward him. "This is a short dissertation on everything I know or can speculate about Mothership Gaia. Unfortunately, it's more speculation than anything else."

Nicolau raised an eyebrow. "Thank you, Jai Li. This is more than I hoped for."

She resisted the urge to shrug his praise away, knowing it was earned. "I want to know, too. Everyone wants to know what happened to her. And if the queens know, well, I want to know why they're not telling."

## II

### KATO: *QUEENSHIP SELVANS*

KATO WASN'T sure he was breathing anymore. The sheer depth of Selvans' power wasted him. His sense of space sprang from light-years to centimeters and back with the slightest nudge. Every person on board breathed the air in his body. No, Selvans' body. Kato struggled to divide the two. Selvans carried his mind along, and Kato felt too small in comparison. What did a queenship need with him? With any pilot?

An array of complex ships bloomed across his awareness: a dozen different queens each with a hundred thousand different drones. They faded away to their places in a multidimensional display that Kato recognized. He could make sense of this war table—the moves each player was likely to make.

The queenships could carry humanity to the edges of the known universe, but it was the human pilots who gave the queens their direction. And it was the pilots who were willing to go to war.

Kato focused on Queenship Lempo, and her image expanded in the war table. He saw Selvans floating beside her, dwarfed by Lempo's moon-sized mass. And yet, dwarfing the cloud of kings and drones that called Lempo home. This image moved in real time. Kato focused closer, into Selvans. Into the heart of the ship where he was standing. Into the cockpit. He wasn't alone.

A rapid heartbeat stood next to Kato. Then he felt a physical hand on his, and the double/triple echo of awareness nauseated him. Kato backed out of the war table and breathed. He found a corner of Selvans' mind open to him that hadn't been before. A complex series of edges—maze-like and knotted—moved and extended to him, and Kato received the distinct impression of a handshake.

Then Selvans' mind surged, and Kato realized this was the man in the room with him. This area was not Selvans; this mind was another person. He hesitated to shake his hand, remembering how easily he fell into Reza's head. Selvans surged again, and Kato felt awash in too much information, beached like a whale. He sensed the stranger weather her volatility much better than he and was impressed.

Only then did it occur to Kato that no one but the pilot should have access to this room, and if he was the pilot... who was this?

## MAS'UD: QUEENSHIP SELVANS

MAS'UD FOUND his connection with Selvans unfolded exponentially when his hand came to rest on the console with the pilot's. He saw their precise location and movement through space, their orientation to the galactic core, and the proximity of every other queenship in the galaxy. He shunted the information to one side, filtering away the details of Selvans' existence to focus on her connection to the pilot.

The line dividing ship from human was indistinct and in flux. Mas'ud couldn't tell if that was by design or indicated a lack of practice. Selvans' every thought—and there were thousands of them per second—flickered through that indistinct place, catching or moving on at random. While Mas'ud's experience was like a boat—self-contained—this felt more like the meeting of two different oceans. Eventually, the larger would swallow the smaller whole.

Mas'ud echoed Pilot Farai's gesture, extending a piece of himself like a greeting, but he received no response. Selvans' desire to bring them together pushed at Mas'ud like an incoming storm. He resisted. If the pilot didn't want to greet him, that was his choice.

But Mas'ud sensed the flexible mind of the pilot churning under Selvans' agitation. He urged her to still. To calm. The storm abated.

Mas'ud extended his greeting again and was pleased when the pilot met him. Kato Ozark, grandchild of Pilot Farai. Delighted, Mas'ud threw his emotion toward Selvans, and the three mingled together. No mental walls kept Kato separate, and even the most surface understanding of the man—heir, soldier, strategist—put Mas'ud in awe. He gushed, *I'm pleased to meet you.*

Direct thoughts were harder for the pilot to form. Mas'ud felt the flowing mind struggle to focus. He pushed at Selvans again: *back away. Relax.* The queenship obeyed.

*Why are you here?*

Mas'ud shrugged and felt the gesture transfer from one mind to another. *Selvans brought me here.*

Then the queenship couldn't be contained any longer. Her greater mind tumbled them together, and Mas'ud lost himself in the tangle for a moment. She spoke. *You both are my pilots. You are here to guide this ship.*

Well, that didn't make any sense. Mas'ud felt the smoke-pieces of Kato's mind startle and then abruptly become mute, as if he stood on another ship, or even planet-side. Mas'ud couldn't feel the pilot's hand anymore. Selvans' joy faded to concern.

## ESHA: *CENTRAL-WARP STATION*

ESHA KALLURI gave her pilots a new target. Her orders cascaded through the system. Bright red trajectories crisscrossed her screens. She pushed them aside. The AI replaced her visuals with numbers—four hundred drones and thirty-six kings. The entire complement of the Vanetta Queenship Ningal harassed her space station and they refused to speak with her. She couldn't even pick the ship up on any of the Crane Central-Warp Station sensors. It was too far out.

A ping came back from her first automated scout: negative. The distance delayed her reports by nearly twenty minutes. Even if she stumbled across the family's queen, they'd be long gone before she ever received the information.

A Tsui mediator could get them to talk, but Esha already knew what they wanted: control of Crane's station. It put Vanetta in a strange spot. They sent their kings and their drones to take potshots at Crane's fighters and strike glancing blows on the outer edges of the station, but they didn't want to risk significant damage to the warp generators. So Esha's fighters flew circles around them, picking off their more-numerous enemy one at a time and salvaging the wreckages for parts to repair the station.

Squad seven docked; their arrival automatically triggered a wave of repair costs against the station's reserves. Two ships didn't check in. Squad fourteen launched their freshly prepped fighters—six pilots down from a full complement. Esha rubbed her face and sent another communication request to the Vanetta queen.

After three months of harassment, she was running out of ideas.

A sudden electrical wash of blue-green lit up Esha's office. It slanted in through the windows on her right. Just beyond her observation deck, an Ozark collector-class drone paid the Crane station a transport fee and stretched through the warp field. The credit covered squad seven's repairs. The warp field evaporated and took the drone with it.

A call blinked on her screen. Esha tapped her first engineer's image. The woman grinned, too close to the screen, as she wrenched it around to display a beat-up fighter vessel. Esha leaned forward. "Show me."

The image jerked, someone tapped on the slate, and the fighter vanished. Not just cloaked in reflection, but truly bending light from every direction. Esha watched a cart maneuver around the back of the ship via guide-line with only the slightest distortion.

"It's not perfect." The first engineer wrenched her screen back around. "But it's nearly invisible on every scanner we have. I'm going to work with Ryan to tweak the thermal—"

"No. If it can fly, I want to send it out right now."

The engineer nodded. "It can fly. It'll do its job. It might get caught on the approach."

"How's work on number two?"

"On schedule."

"Apply your tweaks there. Clear the deck and launch number one. With any luck we won't need a second."

"Yes, ma'am."

Esha closed the call and reviewed her targets. Most of her fighters swarmed Vanetta kingships. Kill the king, and the drones it commanded would transfer to another. But in that moment of transfer, station defenses could pick them off. At least, it had worked the first few times. Now the kings ran back to their queenship, just a warp-step away in some unknown direction.

Her AI marked the launch of the cloaked fighter. Esha gave it a king target and called several pilots off. They all converged on a different king, both as distraction and diversion. The cloaked ship inverted below its target, matched the vector, and magnetized.

Esha redirected her pilots. Harass the target, but let it get away. The kingship swerved through space, but if they noticed an extra two percent of mass, she couldn't tell.

Her office lit up blue-green. A Dhar collector-class drone paid for passage. The Vanetta king warped to its queen.

Esha canceled Dhar's galactic-center warp and opened a jump to new coordinates. Her computer calculated the bend in space and estimated the energy requirement. An alert blinked. The station wasn't oriented correctly for this jump to be efficient. She cleared the warning and activated the jump anyway. Her office darkened and then flooded with light. She directed every fighter through the breach. Three months was enough. Crane didn't have a queenship to rival the other families, but Esha demanded their respect regardless.

Vanetta drones blinked back to Ningal. The enemy numbers on Esha's screen trickled down.

# III

KATO FLOATED away from Selvans' console. He rubbed his neck and stared at Mas'ud. One pilot per ship. Only a single person could integrate at a time. He'd never heard of two, and he wavered between disbelief and anger. He'd hardly processed that he was a pilot, and now he had to share the title?

Mas'ud pulled his broad, olive-toned hand away from the ship. Kato saw awe in his eyes. He tipped toward anger. "Why are you here?"

Mas'ud held up both hands. A class ring decorated one of his fingers. "The ship brought me here. I don't understand why. I'm supposed to be in—"

"Engineering." Kato finished for him. He should have recognized the bronze bars sooner. "You're the first engineer."

"Mas'ud Tavana. At your service." He held his hand out for a proper physical handshake, and Kato took it before he could overthink the gesture. He felt his mind lean into Mas'ud, but the man pushed back, and they found psychic equilibrium. Then, the handshake was just a touch and nothing more.

31

Kato squeezed Mas'ud's hand a bit harder, impressed despite himself. "Selvans said you're a pilot. Did you serve before you got your degree?"

Mas'ud tugged his hand away from Kato's. Immediately Kato's sense of Mas'ud distanced. He found he didn't like the void between them. Kato missed the meeting of their minds. "There's been a mistake. I studied at Dhar University, on Mars—"

"Your ring is Ozark." Kato frowned. He wasn't aware that anyone affiliated with Dhar would have been allowed on the ship, less promoted to first engineer.

Mas'ud twisted the ring with his thumb. "I got my first degree at Dhar. I received my second at U of Ozark, earthside, when the first one wasn't enough to get me onto a queen. I know biomechanical systems and repair, crystal composite structures, and I can design anything." He offered a barking laugh. "But I'm no pilot."

The ship shuddered around them. Kato pressed his hand to his head and felt her yearn in Mas'ud's direction. "Selvans disagrees."

"I know." Mas'ud knuckled his fist over one temple. "I can hear her. She's persistent. But I don't see how I can help you up here." He made a palm-up gesture at Kato. "I mean... you've been training for this your entire life. Your grandmother. Your mother." Kato frowned, but Mas'ud powered on. "I'm half decent at chess, but commanding an army? At war?"

"We're not at war."

Mas'ud made a complicated face that ended with amused tolerance. "If you want a debate—"

Selvans rose up around them, a mental wave of being that washed them both into the sea of her mind. Kato floundered, but Mas'ud pitched forward as if struck from behind. Kato grabbed him. Their minds touched, and then Selvans cast their awareness out into space.

## Mas'ud: *Queenship Selvans*

Mas'ud stretched thin across space and knew Kato was dragged along with him. While his mind floated, he felt Kato push his body. Mas'ud fell into a chair of some kind. Soft membrane that conformed to his shape. His awareness snapped back into form around a queenship under attack: Vanetta's Queenship Ningal. He felt the size of her, comparable to Selvans, but dense. Older. And confused. Her pilot was dying. She faced a rapidly growing force of Crane fighters and was exposed without her drones and kings. Mas'ud didn't understand— Crane largely kept to themselves, tending the warp gate to the center of the galaxy. Why would they suddenly mount an offensive of this scale?

*We pushed, they're pushing back.* Kato's thought flowed to him, sharp and alert. The ship's perspective changed, and Mas'ud felt Kato flexing control over his view. Space zoomed out, and a marker notated the location of Crane's space station. Four dozen smaller dots traveled in small leapfrogging jumps across the gap, from the space station back to Queenship Ningal. Vanetta's missing kings and drones. "Vanetta has been harassing Crane for months. We have the advantage at the distance."

Mas'ud pulled his view back to Ningal and saw her faltering under the assault. "We?"

"Ozark owns all of Vanetta's assets. They go where we tell them." Kato extended a shaky mental handshake.

Mas'ud met it. Sixty years of political jockeying downloaded into his awareness, layering a simple space skirmish in cause and effect. With a weak-willed pilot and no substantial capital to speak of, Vanetta could easily be overrun by any other family. When they had approached Farai, she ruthlessly negotiated a contract that fell heavily in Ozark's favor. Protection in exchange for political slavery.

Crane wasn't attacking Vanetta. Ozark was attacking Crane. And that Mas'ud could understand. Everyone wanted control of the warp station, and Farai was nothing if not ambitious.

Explosive decompression rocked Ningal's lower portside. Mas'ud felt the rent metal and crystal like a gaping hole in his ribs. Selvans pushed Mas'ud and Kato into Ningal's heart, muscling past the queen's mental walls. Ningal's pilot shuddered and died.

Mas'ud became Queenship Ningal. He was venting atmosphere and portside defenses were off-line. Small fighters swarmed around him—gnats with persistent little bites everywhere at once. A thousand small alarms rang throughout his corridors.

He started with the alarms. Silence, so he could think. He flexed his outer shell and sealed the breach and then squeezed the air away from an internal fire to quench it. The gnats ganged up, punching through his defenses by firing together at one spot. Mas'ud called for his kings and drones, but their voices were too far away. Kato shunted him a calculation: another five minutes until they arrived. Too long. Ningal would be nothing but scrap by then. They needed to jump faster.

Or jump farther.

An idea blossomed, and Selvans' greater mind helped him build it. Mas'ud reached for the distant drones. He molded them together like clay while Selvans secured the people inside, isolating them. Mas'ud stretched the drones thin, breaking and reforming their crystal composite into a large ring. A kingship warped into the area, and he grabbed control of that as well. Two more kingships joined the ring. Mas'ud redirected their energy. The ring vibrated. A warp tunnel splashed open.

Mas'ud left the impromptu ring under Selvans' control and moved his attention back to Ningal. Her distant drones and kings could now jump all the way back to local space. They made the leap in a rush. Kato imposed control over the kings, while Mas'ud snagged the small drones as they arrived. Selvans shunted the people they carried into small emergency capsules that Ningal could absorb.

At their most basic, the variously designed drone ships were a mobile source of raw material. Mas'ud stretched them out into flat plates: thin, wide metal-crystal hybrids. He reinforced Ningal's vulnerable portside with them. Crane's fighters swung about to the fore. Mas'ud grabbed a drone and pulled it into Ningal. The ship crashed through two fighters and broke into dozens of sharp pieces. He pushed the pieces back out, and like javelin they pierced another six fighters. They listed in space, drifting without direction from a pilot.

With Mas'ud in control of shape and form, the Crane fighters lost some of their human-controlled advantage. Mas'ud could retrieve and reshape any piece of Ningal. The queenship herself struggled to act beyond internal repairs. Without the flexibility of a human mind to guide her, the ship lacked strategic decision-making skills.

Kato fought the battle for her. He touched the king-ships gently, organizing squadrons and teams. He guid-ed them in looping arcs around Ningal, using her massive size to break line of sight or ambush Crane fighters. Mas'ud felt the kings orbit him and sent shards of drone crystals spinning in the same direction. The entire battlefield rotated clockwise. Crane fighters flying against the debris field disintegrated.

The remaining fighters suddenly disengaged. Kato's kings chased them some distance away until they warped out of local space. Mas'ud tracked their jump following a vector back to the station.

It was over.

Mas'ud prompted Ningal to check herself. He patched atmosphere leaks, repaired corridors, and healed fractured crystals. As he mended the ship, he pulled at her shape, morphing the queen into a sleek, long cylinder with a blunt nose. He cavitated the back end, breaking apart her ability to warp, and then reformed the engines in a central ring. He recalled all the shrapnel orbiting the ship, reforming some drones from the scrap, and using other pieces as raw material to rebuild. Mas'ud unlocked newly molded docking ports. Ningal's kingships came home.

The queen searched the people she housed and selected a new pilot. Mas'ud let his mental grip relax. The queenship slipped from his control. Selvans cradled him back across the gulf of space where his mind folded back into his own body—like returning too much taffy into its package.

Mas'ud was enclosed somewhere warm and comfortable. He couldn't see, but he heard a rhythmic and low double-thump like a heartbeat. His stretched mind slowly retracted, adjusting to his small and limited physical body. He took a deep breath and pushed his hand forward. The membrane flowered open to the light.

## LaRay: Queenship Demeter

Queenship Demeter moved her pawn up one space, threatening LaRay's bishop. LaRay couldn't say she was an expert at the game, but she spent a moment considering the new move.

Rudo leaned toward her. "Tsui just broadcast an update on the McLaren-Crane talks."

LaRay hummed. "Let me guess, Tsui has successfully brokered a nonmilitarized zone and is optimistic..." She waved her hand to indicate additional legalese.

"Not at all." Rudo smiled, an expression full of teeth. "Talks exploded. Literally. The Tsui are blaming McLaren radicals. Fighting broke out in pockets across the city, and it sounds like at least two simultaneous attacks have crippled Paomia's emergency response abilities."

"McLaren's warring against Tsui?" LaRay frowned at her daughter.

"I don't think so. They may just be a means to an end. When was the last time McLaren agreed to an uncontested border?"

"It has to be at least twenty years."

Rudo nodded. "I bet they're not getting anything out of these talks. It was just a way to take out a few of Crane's decision makers. Tsui casualties are a side effect."

"Interesting."

"Has Tsui asked for help?"

"No, but they won't. They wouldn't risk putting themselves in debt to another family unless it was a last resort." LaRay spread her fingers out on the surface of her desk. Its composite crystal hummed under her touch. Demeter met her mind through the connection and verified she could make the move in a single jump. LaRay traveled the short mental distance to her bridge. She pushed her thoughts at her first commander.

*Commander Sahar, bring us in to Paomia.*

She released Demeter before Sahar could acknowledge the order, and addressed Rudo. "It's about time we extended an offer ourselves, though."

A breath later Demeter's pleasant voice permeated the ship. *Warp in twenty seconds*.

Rudo wrinkled her nose but made no comment. Tsui-owned Paomia orbited a double neutron star, spinward, and closer to the center than Demeter's current position. Paomia was one of six moons around a gas giant, the clouds of which Tsui harvested for nitrogen and molecular water.

*Warp in ten seconds.*

LaRay reached through Demeter to contact the closest Tsui queenship. Qu Yuan acknowledged the handshake but her pilot didn't.

*Warp in five. Four. Three. Two. One. Prepare for jump.*

Rudo's complexion turned an odd shade of green. She excused herself to the bathroom.

Pilot Maylin's greeting was a hard assault. *Be brief. Why are you here?*

LaRay gentled her mental touch. *To offer support. Supplies, personnel, first aid, refugee space, anything you need.*

Maylin's contact bristled. *Dhar won't receive anything in return.*

*I'm not asking for reparation, Maylin. We're here for emergency response. I'm sending down a hospital drone as we speak. What else does Paomia need to get back on their feet?*

LaRay felt Maylin's mind retreat, a psychic distance indicating her attention had moved away. LaRay considered the chessboard on her slate. She moved her castle to threaten Demeter's last horse. Would that scare her away from taking the bishop?

When Maylin returned it was with a list. LaRay pushed it to the bridge without reviewing it. The supplies were irrelevant to her. *Has McLaren left you with any indication they're willing to talk?*

*I'm not going to comment on ongoing negotiations.*

*So you haven't kicked them from the table.*

Maylin's anger leaked through like sap squeezing be-tween cracks, and it seemed her tone was directed at McLaren. *It's in everyone's interest to resolve the border dispute.*

*Is it? McLaren's pressure has kept Crane's gate open to any family that can afford the jump.*

Maylin didn't laugh, but her thoughts lightened. *Tsui is in good standing with Crane, LaRay. If you need another family to bully them into doing business with you, perhaps you should take this time to improve your relations with Crane rather than goodwill your way into our favor.* Her mind distanced. *Thank you for your donations, by the way. We do appreciate the assistance.* Then her wall came up, and LaRay was left at the door.

Rudo floated by her desk, sipping on a tea bulb. Her braids drifted around her shoulders. "What's the word on McLaren?"

"Tsui's going to continue negotiating. I doubt they'll invite anyone back to Paomia, though. We're likely the last ones to visit here for a while."

Rudo straightened. "I'll get on the next drone going planetside. Have they given us a deadline?" She pushed away from the desk and reached to the ceiling for a tie-down.

"Not yet." LaRay checked the supplies list on her slate. "See if you can't find Trai Le while you're down there. Lawyer. He and I have had more than a few fruitful talks. You might be able to get more out of him than Maylin was willing to say."

Not that LaRay expected much more from Maylin. She embodied Tsui's neutral stance in all things and would do well leading the family when her aunt passed.

Demeter took LaRay's bishop. LaRay took her queenship's horse. *Checkmate in three moves,* she said.

## IV

## KATO: *QUEENSHIP SELVANS*

KATO LURCHED from Selvans' embrace. He shielded his eyes against the light and debated with his stomach over the merits of vomiting. His head felt too big for his skull, as if his mind still floated in the vastness of space while his body stumbled about like a blind infant. The nausea and disassociation passed. Kato's reluctance to reengage with his queenship did not.

Mas'ud's hand thrust up to the light, and Selvans retracted the membrane cocooning him. Kato grabbed his hand and helped pull him up, cradling his head in one hand. Mas'ud turned into his touch. "Ugh, that's a rough transition." He kept his eyes closed.

Kato considered his copilot silently. While Kato knew a thing or two about military tactics, it was hard-won familiarity. Studying, practicing, simulating battles until his eyes watered. Kato had spent more than one night cramming before an exam, scratching out his place within Ozark. He'd earned the title.

But Mas'ud's talent for manipulating the ship designs came to him like breathing. Kato had seen Queenship Ningal give up her control in the face of Mas'ud's absolute skill. Kato knew there were better candidates

43

to be pilot. He hadn't even made the shortlist. Why was he here?

Mas'ud wrinkled his nose and gave Kato's shoulder a weak pat. "Selvans, calm down. Give me some space."

The membranous room around them flexed and released like a sigh. Kato breathed a laugh. "I think you're right. This ship has made a mistake."

Mas'ud squinted one eye open. "I'm glad we're on the same page." He took a deep breath and reached for a tie-down in the ceiling. "I should get back to Engineering."

Kato squeezed Mas'ud's hand. "You belong in this room more than me."

"Ha-ha." Mas'ud slid his eyes across Kato's face and sobered. "You're not joking."

Kato lifted his eyebrows. "You don't see it?"

"I'm an engineer, Kato. I can build things. You're the one who just defeated Crane with half a squadron of kings and some tactical ballet."

"I had a little help."

"I threw rocks." Mas'ud's smile only lifted one corner of his mouth.

Kato wanted to see a proper grin in its place. "You built a mobile warpgate on the fly and re-designed an entire queenship mid-battle."

Mas'ud scoffed. "I didn't design anything. Ningal was using a layout that was decades old. The bullet ship design is more practical for mid-distance assault. The drones are easier to... what are you smiling at?"

Kato grabbed Mas'ud's shoulders. "You rebuilt Vanetta's only queenship from the inside out in—" Kato checked the watch on his wrist. "—About two hours. There is an honest-to-god queenship flying in space right now with your fingerprints all over it. That wasn't a simulation."

Mas'ud's eyes bugged. He said quietly, "Oh, shit."

"You're Selvans' pilot." Kato let him go.

Mas'ud gripped his hand and they drifted closer. "No. I can't be. I don't know the first thing about politics. All that information about Ozark owning Vanetta's assets—that was all you. And you're the one with the military background—"

"Which you can learn—"

"No—"

Selvans' mind crashed over them both, a heavy wave demanding attention. *You are both my pilots.*

Mas'ud reeled from the psychic impact. Kato hugged him closer. They both breathed in each other's ears.

"Well, shit," Kato said.

Mas'ud pressed his forehead to Kato's shoulder and groaned. "I need to get back to Engineering."

Kato stiffened. "I'm not doing this without you."

"Fine." Mas'ud pulled away. "But this wasn't exactly on my to-do list, you know. I need some time." He let out a rough bark of a laugh. "I'm supposed to be organizing optimum ship designs for submission to the pilot."

Kato let him go. "It's probably time I had a real sit-down with Reza, anyway."

"Who?"

"The First Commander Ahmad."

"Right…" Mas'ud shook his head, serious again. "Right." The wall irised open and Mas'ud pulled himself through. Kato paused at the open doorway and pressed his palm to the membrane ceiling. He felt Selvans' satisfaction pulsing around the room. A quieter beat followed Mas'ud down the hall and Kato could sense him even after he turned a corner out of sight.

"Sir?" Kato looked down at a security guard stationed outside the room. "Sir, who was that?"

"That was Pilot Mas'ud Tavana and you will accord him due respect."

The soldier straightened. "Yes, sir. And, your title, sir?"

Kato pulled himself into the hall. "I'm Pilot Kato Ozark. We both command this ship."

"Yes, sir…"

## MAS'UD: *QUEENSHIP SELVANS*

SELVANS THROBBED in Mas'ud's head, a celebration of joy/excitement/multitudes. He floated down the halls, experiencing her in flashes of more minute detail with every touch of his hand to composite crystal. His thoughts swam. They intersected with Selvans and broke free again, flowing without rhythm. The queenship's attention dotted around herself, first in the bridge, and then to the galley, down to a dark space in her gut where Mas'ud couldn't make sense of what she showed him but felt profound anticipation.

He swung into the operations hall and pushed her mind away. This new title only changed his entire life plan. He wanted a chance to focus!

He was briefly thankful Kato seemed to have the practical side of piloting under control. Amala could stand in Mas'ud's place in a pinch, but she was no more suited to sudden promotion than he. They hadn't even settled into their rooms yet.

But Mas'ud could appreciate Kato feeling out of his depth. Even if the man was far more qualified than Mas'ud, the sudden immenseness of Selvans required wary respect. She was a barely contained solar storm. It wouldn't take more than a thought to wipe clean every human consciousness on this ship like so much electronic static.

Mas'ud grabbed a tie-down at the doorway to Engineering. He braced on the wall. Selvans pulsed disbelief and offense at his thought of her nuking her human population. Mas'ud squinted. "I want some privacy in my own head, Selvans."

The chitchat in Engineering scratched to a stop. Amala trailed her fingers down the edge of her head-scarf as if tucking hair behind her ear. She cleared her throat. "Sorry?"

"Nothing." Mas'ud pulled himself into the room. "How are all of your design ideas coming?"

Zola perked up. "I'm having fun with mine."

"Where did you start?"

Amala said, "Put it up on the screen."

"Well"—Zola shared her design on the wall screen and floated over to describe it—"you said we needed to get all our ships out as fast as possible. That means every ship has its own bay. But you can't just make the queen longer, it'll take a year to get from one end to the other."

"Your solution looks very geometric." Mas'ud observed.

"It is. I looked up the latest molecular designs with the most interior surface area. In micro, we can use these patterns to hold huge quantities of gas in a compact space, but in macro..." Zola zoomed the image closer and each interlinked bar resolved into a complete shuttle bay with mass transit moving people down a center spine. "We can simulate the shape while customizing individual bays. Larger drones can dock on the outer edges while smaller ones fit the inner spaces."

Ismet said, "Huh. That's smart."

Zola beamed.

"Why isn't this kind of thing used already?"

Amala traced the repeating triangular structure. "Warp rings need to be round and pushing a queenship to build from circular in one area to triangles in another is very difficult. Pilots don't have absolute control over their ships. If a queen doesn't want to be triangles, she isn't going to be."

Mas'ud felt Selvans reject the notion. He crossed his arms. "I'm not sure that's the whole story. Not every pilot prioritizes drones and kings in flight. Take Queen Lempo. Farai doesn't have a warp ring since she needs to stay in Earth's orbit. Lempo could be a giant pyramid if she wanted."

"But wasn't the moon round?" Zola asked.

Mas'ud shrugged. "Sure. But mass is the same no matter what shape it takes. Lempo isn't round for nostalgia's sake. It's the easiest way to condense all the required mass into a space smaller than Jupiter. Even then, the composite that makes up a queenship isn't as dense as the moon was, so Lempo's almost the same size as Earth in order to generate the same gravitational effects."

Zola gazed at her design on the screen. "So Selvans could be circular at one end and triangular at the other?"

"I'll try it tomorrow and let you know. Who's next?"

"Me." Ismet touched his hand slate to the wall and put his image on the screen. "Space is basically a fluid, so I looked up some deep-sea creatures for inspiration..."

Amala leaned over Zola's slate, pointing at something. She spoke quietly and picked up the phone. Selvans stretched toward her so that he could listen in. Mas'ud jerked his attention back to Ismet's fin design.

## ESHA: *CENTRAL-WARP STATION*

AT CRANE Central-Warp Station, a Dhar collector-class drone with the maximum allowable diameter and the length of twelve kings requested passage. Esha's office remained dark. A ping on her slate blinked red. She called the drone. "Sorry, Dhar. Looks like you're out of credits."

A confusion of voices burst back at her. The only one she heard distinctly yelled, "The third time this quarter!"

"You can bring it up with Mx. Crane if you think there's a mistake."

"We'll pay you double."

Esha made a note of the offer against their drone's ID. Mx. Crane had more use of their disloyalty than Esha had of their money. "I'll pocket the tip, say thank you, and you still won't get through. No credit, no warp."

"Yeah, shit. Are we in negotiations with you?"

Esha queried the database. Crane was always in negotiations with someone.

## ADILA: *CENTRAL-WARP STATION OFFICES*

ADILA CRANE huffed. "Don't drag this conversation in circles, Nicolau. We've always ever required payment for a service—"

"It's a tithe, and Dhar isn't going to stand for it." The man glowered from behind his desk and ego.

Adila tapped a small screen-in-screen box on her slate. The crisp, dimensioned image transferred briefly to their mediator Maylin Tsui who looked as aloof and put together as always. That cultivated look always inspired Adila. Calm under pressure. She tapped back to Nicolau.

"The sums are outrageous. Are you trying to bankrupt us?"

Adila leaned forward. "If you want lower charges, I need to see some support from Dhar. Second to AC-C, we're the most contested location in the galaxy. Without a queen and pilot to rebuild we're using good old-fashioned elbow grease." She didn't expect Nicolau would know manual work if it bit him in the well-dressed ass.

Nicolau made a rare curl across his lips. "Ozark has more access than we d—"

"Ozark doesn't harass us on Earth. We appreciate their restraint."

"We don't harass you on Earth."

Adila's laugh was dry. "No, only here at the warp station."

"Dammit, Adila—"

Maylin's smooth-featured image cut Nicolau's audio off, and Adila knew he was seeing the same thing. "Mx. Crane, does Crane have any unmet needs Dhar may be able to fill in place of cash payment?"

"Hmm." She tapped Nicolau's image to reconnect them. He reclined in his chair and managed a look that said he was above this peasant dispute. "McLaren has been expanding their station network against our borders. They expand at Dhar's request."

Nicolau barked, "If we had access we wouldn't need McLaren—"

"So you admit you're encouraging them to pressure us."

"You halved our credits last quarter!"

"Because you tried to—" Adila cut herself off and jabbed Maylin's image. The projection of Nicolau behind his desk receded. Their mediator took his place. Adila huffed and settled again. "If Dhar agrees to pull McLaren back, we'll reinstate their credit limit at fifteen hundred effective tomorrow. We'll issue ten credits immediately in good faith and roll up to the limit over the rest of the quarter should they keep McLaren at a distance."

Maylin nodded at her and the screen blanked to Tsui's family logo. The background subtly blended from one shade of neutral tan to another while Adila waited. When Maylin returned, a list with Nicolau's counteroffer scrolled beside her: seventy immediate round-trip credits in exchange for McLaren pulling back two light-years.

Adila frowned. The number of trips she credited to Dhar was irrelevant—it was just something to argue over while they debated the real problem: McLaren. To a family with a queen, two light-years was next door. She couldn't let them take half a step back only to jump forward at the next dispute.

"Not good enough." She pulled a map up beside Maylin's image and shared the display. "Thirty immediate round-trips. For every light-year McLaren pulls these stations back"—Adila mapped four movement directions for four different McLaren stations—"we'll grant another seven hundred warps. No limit. And later, for every light-year they drift closer, they'll lose a thousand."

Maylin considered the terms. "This will not echo well in your talks with McLaren."

"If Nicolau agrees to this, we won't need to continue talks with McLaren. Dhar will manage them to stay in our good graces."

Maylin tapped her screen and left Adila with the Tsui logo. She checked the clock. Nicolau's neutral expression popped back onto her screen in less than thirty seconds. Adila smothered a smile. She'd won. Gloating didn't become a lady.

"We'll go through thirty trips in a day." Nicolau's protest was for show. His lack of counteroffer said he intended to agree to her terms.

"Then I suggest you get McLaren on the phone."

He wrinkled his nose briefly. "To overrun your little space station? That's a good idea."

Adila cocked her head to the side. "Nicolau, if you so much as breathed the thought of attacking us in full force, every queenship in local space would warp in to stop you. Just call off your guard dog. We'll give you what you want."

Nicolau's image blipped back to Maylin, but the list of terms flashed green, and the impression of Nicolau's thumbprint faded in at the bottom. Adila pressed her thumb beside it.

## ESHA: CENTRAL-WARP STATION

ESHA'S SLATE pinged green. Dhar's credits jumped from zero to thirty. She called the collector-class drone. "Looks like we have an agreement, but I'll still take that tip if you're offering."

"Only because you're such a great host." The Dhar drone paid for passage and tipped half again. Esha's office flooded with light.

## V

## KATO: *QUEENSHIP SELVANS*

THE SITUATION room encircled a slim, magnetized plate acting as a table surface for Kato's handheld slate. He floated at the head of the row, memorizing the faces before him. Selvans gave him instant background information as he requested it, filling in chain-of-command details, and Kato managed to stay out of everyone's head during the initial round of handshakes.

First Commander Reza completed introductions with Fleet Commander Itzel Olen. Now here was a woman Kato could relate to. With her mother an ambassador and her father serving as Farai's first commander, the Itzel family had heavy expectations—on top of her exemplary career.

Kato didn't need Selvans' laundry list of accomplishments to fill in Itzel's history. He'd grown up hearing her name. Farai always felt competition was required for growth. Kato considered Itzel a fellow prisoner in the political machine rather than the stepping-stone to higher ground his grandmother saw.

He wondered if his own name had been used against her in similar fashion. He couldn't hope to be an unknown—everyone knew the name Kato Ozark for reasons he neither controlled nor approved of—but at least non-hostile was in his grasp, right?

Itzel followed Reza's introduction with a polite nod to Kato's rank. He resisted the urge to use Selvans to delve into her mind, surprised that he'd want to invade at all. Her opinion of him was irrelevant. The regulations of military service made him political king. It wasn't just smart of her to play that game—she had no other choice. So why did he feel like there was a sword dangled on a string overhead?

Reza continued, "The final member of this cabinet is an honorary noncombat position, usually reserved for the pilot's spouse."

Kato hummed. "I'm surprised there are any non-essential roles on this ship."

"It's not considered nonessential. The moral and logistical support of the spouse is often key in maintaining a pilot's well-being over the long-term. You don't exactly have a retirement option." Polite chuckles circled the room.

"I'm not married. Can I select someone to fill the role?" Kato fingered the hem of his shirt sleeve. He needed an ally in this room. Someone who already knew all his secrets and wouldn't judge him.

"And if you get married later?"

"Are you proposing, Commander?"

Reza's cheeks pinked and she said gruffly, "You're hardly tall enough for me."

Kato smiled. "Let's not burn that bridge until we get there, then." He thrust his mind into Selvans and sought Ceren. Selvans located her at the bridge in an instant, doing a job Kato was likely better suited for than any of this. He extended a mental handshake. The ease with which she met it should not have surprised him. There were reasons she was on the short list for piloting.

He requested her at the sit. room immediately.

When she arrived, Reza had just expanded a galactic map onto the big screen. Kato waved her into the room beside him. Reza nodded her acknowledgement and continued to speak, her hand arcing over the anti-spinward arm on display. "Ozark informally owns a number of systems on the edge of the galaxy. We tithe semiannually, but except for an occasional trade drone, Ozark has little presence out here."

Ceren leaned close to Kato. "Why do they pay tithes if they are informal ownerships?"

"They're still registered as independent systems."

"So they're illegal."

"Informal sounds better."

"Am I really supposed to be your moral compass?"

"Yep."

She snorted softly. "Boy, you sure can pick 'em."

Reza cleared her throat and Kato jumped. "Something you kids want to share with the class?"

"Yes, actually." Ceren straightened, eyes bright. "Is it safe to assume that other families with queens will also have informal ownerships around the galaxy?"

Reza slid a look to Kato that he interpreted as bemused approval. There was no way Ceren would be content with "honorary." "Yes, that's a safe guess." She swiped the screen and made a selection. Dots of color populated their view of the spiral arm. "Here are the registered ownerships. They largely fall in line with the known territory claims." She turned a digital dial. Colors faded out and new dots took their places. This collection showed no regard for territory. "These are the informal ownerships we're confident about. We have varying levels of surety for another few hundred that muddle the water further."

Kato shook his head at the display. "Are there any neutral systems left?"

"With populations?"

He nodded.

"Do you consider Tsui neutral?"

Ceren said, "No."

"Good." And Reza smiled. She turned the digital dial again. A single system glowed white. "This is Pru system. They have three gas giants with several habitable moons. They are tithed by no one, registered by no one, and have no direct trade with any family."

"What do they have?" Kato asked.

"Warpgate technology powered by their binary sun system."

Itzel leaned forward. "It works?"

"We believe so."

"Is it mobile?"

"Unlikely."

Ceren turned to Kato. "How much hydrogen does it take to maintain a warpgate?"

Selvans provided numbers before he could admit he didn't know. He balked at it. "A few trillion cubic meters per second. Crane's Central-Warp is the biggest. Values drop with the size."

"I don't have any context for that size."

Reza said, "All the hydrogen in Sol's Jupiter could power Central-Warp for a day."

Ceren shook her head as she gazed at the softly glowing dot that was Pru. "This is where we're headed, isn't it?"

"I'll eat my shirt if it isn't," Kato muttered. Selvans' mind surged then, and he had to fight out from under it. He squinted at Reza, trying to make out her words. He thought he heard Mas'ud's voice cry out his name. Then Selvans yanked him from his own head and put him in a ceiling.

The change in perspective nauseated him, but the chaos he saw in what had to be Engineering twisted his gut in altogether new ways. A woman in a headscarf was yelling, alternating her attention from Mas'ud, to a man in white, and back again. Then, a scuffle. A syringe. Mas'ud's mind flashed red anger and immediately muted to pink.

Kato lurched forward in the sit. room, interrupting conversation. He yanked himself to the exit. Ceren called after him, "What's going on?"

"Mas'ud," was all he said.

Before the door irised closed behind him, he heard Reza ask, "Who?" There hadn't been a good time to bring up Mas'ud's name during the briefing. He pushed himself down the hall toward Engineering, but cast his mind back to Reza—through Selvans—for a rough mental handshake. She took it. He all but threw his memory at her: the introduction to Selvans' heart, the way Mas'ud sailed Selvans' mind like he was born to it, the Vanetta queen's nearly disastrous encounter with Crane—Oh, she wasn't happy he'd kept that from her, but it wasn't as if he'd been hiding it. He'd just gotten wrapped up!

He growled around a corner, and by the time he made it to Engineering, Kato was furious. At least the dull, muted throb that was Mas'ud's mind in his head was a problem he could solve. He hit the doorway hard. "What the hell is going on in here?"

Surprised silence greeted him. Mas'ud floated mid-room, nearly catatonic. The man in white—a doctor, now that Kato saw him from the right angle—still held the syringe. Kato tensed. In response, composite crystal from the floor and ceiling shot into the room and bound the doctor where he was. Everyone jumped and pushed themselves away. Kato smothered his surprise. He hadn't meant to do that. Selvans was reacting to his raw emotion. The woman in a headscarf eyed him. "You're the pilot?"

Kato swallowed his first angry reply. It wasn't helpful. "Kato Ozark. I'm taking Mas'ud." He pushed into the room and spared a moment to glare at the doc.

"He needs help," the woman said. "He wandered off without explanation, and he's been saying odd things since he returned."

"What kinds of odd things?"

A younger woman floating at the side of the room spoke up. "He said he'd try to make the ship triangular."

Kato didn't know what good that would do, but he wasn't an engineer. Selvans sent him a complicated sense-image he didn't care to study. "Well he's the pilot. He can do that."

The woman in the headscarf narrowed her eyes. "I thought you were the pilot?" Her hostile attention rolled with complex anger and fear. Selvans had access to her mind. She was scared for Mas'ud.

Kato closed his eyes for a moment. They needed to have a ship-wide announcement on chain of command. "We're both Selvans' pilots." He pinned the doctor with a glare. "What did you give him?"

The man wisely wasn't struggling in his crystal prison. "Just a sedative, sir. It's light."

Kato drifted close enough to grip Mas'ud's arm. The physical connection deepened Kato's mental one. Mas'ud twitched under his grip. Kato saw his eyes try to focus and fail. "How long until it wears off?"

"A few hours."

Kato wrapped his arm around Mas'ud's chest and tugged him close. "I'm taking him," he said again. Though he wasn't sure where, exactly. His quarters were nowhere near here, and he couldn't pull a semi-conscious man through the corridors. Still, no one tried to stop him, and that counted for something.

Selvans tugged him left, and he followed the feeling. They traveled deeper into the ship, but only a few corridors inward, when a door irised open. Mas'ud's quarters.

Finally alone, Kato could get a better look at his co-pilot. Mas'ud's eyes drifted, and he didn't appear to have any muscle control. Or he just didn't care at the moment. He floated passively in Kato's arms.

Kato tilted his head up. "Mas'ud can you hear me? It's Kato." He pushed his mind close, but Mas'ud was all gray clouds and mist. "I'm going to strap you into bed. Just sleep this off for a few hours. You're going to be fine."

He tugged Mas'ud to the wall bay and harnessed him in. He pulled on the straps and checked that nothing pinched.

"Ay-tohh?"

Kato floated up to look at Mas'ud's face.

The man smiled at him, lopsided and drunk. He whispered, quite clearly, "You're cute."

Heat unexpectedly crawled up Kato's neck, and he looked away.

"Thought, maybe, dinner... before tucking me in."

Kato laughed. "Sleep, Mas'ud. Selvans will tell me when you're awake, and then we'll do dinner."

"Good-night... kiss?"

Kato pushed away from the wall.

"Kinda... prince... are you?"

Kato bit his lip as the door irised closed behind him. It could have been funny: Kato, prince charming; Mas'ud, lord in distress. Except Kato was already heir to too many thrones, and even his copilot's semiconscious joke was too close to the truth.

## MAS'UD: *QUEENSHIP SELVANS*

IN RETROSPECT, it may have been a good idea to mention to his coworkers that he'd been chosen by the ship to help pilot. Mas'ud couldn't fault Amala for calling a doctor—that's exactly what he would have done given the circumstances. He owed her an apology. And not some mental message sent via queenship, but a proper face-to-face talk with contrite puppy-eyes and everything.

Selvans offered to remind him the next time he saw her, but he doubted he would forget. He was in for a lashing he well deserved.

There were enough unfamiliar faces around the room that Mas'ud already relied on Selvans more than he liked. The ship was like instant-access internet in his head.

A dozen men and women circled the table in full dress, bars of color on their breasts indicating how vastly outranked Mas'ud really was. Even Kato had a few bars on his blues. At one end of the room, a tall woman brought a corner of the galaxy up on screen. She rattled off names around the room for Mas'ud's benefit, though he knew more through Selvans than the woman provided.

Itzel Olen: Fleet commander and practiced tactician. Leads her class in simulations for swift and effective combat, though not always with the fewest casualties.

Ceren Karga: Valedictorian and Earth-born. Not directly descended from a family, but friends in the right circles gave her privilege by association.

Reza Ahmadi: First commander. The woman in charge should Selvans lose her pilots.

The queenship knew an inordinate amount of personal information that Mas'ud was uncomfortable having access to. It made him wonder how the ship discovered it all. Did she hold every detail about his life?

Did Kato know?

His drugged teasing with Kato hours ago took on a new light, and he mentally shied away from the ocean connection to Selvans. Was it too late to keep any parts of his life private?

Beside him, Kato looked up, alert, seeking. Their eyes met, and Kato's mind reached for his. Mas'ud didn't shake hands. How was he supposed to keep himself separate if Selvans could offer everything he was on a platter?

Reza launched into what Mas'ud suspected was a rehash of information these people had already heard. Apparently his earlier encounter with the doc had put the entire meeting on hold. With Mas'ud now more widely known as a pilot, he was required to attend.

Kato leaned in and whispered, "You sure the sedative is worn off?"

Mas'ud nodded. "It was a little foggy there for a while. But I'm all right."

There was a pause, and then Mas'ud sensed Kato's mind retreat. "I'm not... trying to read anyone's mind." Kato worked the edge of his sleeve and spoke quietly.

"She's all rolling and tempest. I feel like I'm just floating along... Sometimes I'm drowning. Emotions are passed through me like I'm a convenient conduit. Sometimes I'm not sure who they're from."

Mas'ud touched his hand to the desk. "Who can you hear?"

Kato cast his gaze around the room. "You. Reza. Ceren. On some level, anyone who's in contact with the ship herself." Kato turned to look at Mas'ud's hand.

Mas'ud resisted the urge to move it out of sight. He mentally reached for Kato instead. Their handshake melded, and Mas'ud walled Selvans off as much as he could. He couldn't silence her storm, but maybe he could build a small shelter.

He sensed Kato's immediate relaxation. The tension around his eyes eased, and some of the nervous hum occupying his mind released. From the safety of their mental life raft, Kato admitted, *It's impressive how easily you do this. I remain convinced you're the right choice for pilot.*

Mas'ud shifted and frowned. He ran his finger under the strap holding him into the chair. *I used to think that queens chose their pilots deliberately. There was a reason for each one.*

*And now?*

*Now, I think the reason I was chosen is to show you there's a reason you were.* Mas'ud stretched the walls of their life raft, thinning them out. He could sense Selvans' greater mind surging, her rolling waves of information as they were processed and stored among the crystal composite. He could see it, filter it, and stay focused on what was important. He selected Reza's memory of the interrupted briefing.

Informal ownerships. Illegal, as Ceren pointed out. Pru system: unaffiliated, independent, and with a huge bargaining chip. Positioned to become a family in name if their tech worked as rumored.

Mas'ud pulled pieces and chunks of data from Selvans. Pru history, Ozark's history with Pru, its associations with other families, the physical makeup of their system, and economic data that took a sudden weird turn six years ago. He visualized the net of related pieces, and as his image of the situation grew, so did Kato's comfort.

Kato stepped into his picture, touching bits of organized data here and there. He jumped from spot to spot, adding new connections and depth. He highlighted a gap, and Mas'ud pulled from Selvans to fill it. They danced around each other like this for a while, weaving the full tapestry of Ozark's situation.

Even if Pru had a functional solar warp as the data suggested, they weren't a threat to the Ozark. But if McLaren got their hands on a mobile warp, or if Dhar could harness a solar-powered warp, Ozark could well be endangered.

Mas'ud hummed. He reached through Selvans to greet F. C. Ahmadi's mind and watched her jerk. She hesitated with her mental handshake. Mas'ud didn't need it. "I'm sorry to interrupt, but there's no need to review this for my benefit. Let's skip forward to what we're going to do about it."

Reza didn't mind the interruption, but Mas'ud felt her disbelief at his confidence with the situation. "When were you briefed?"

"Just now."

"In the past minute and a half?"

Kato said, "Yes."

And after a tense moment, that was the end of it. Reza zoomed her display in on Pru. Mas'ud asked, "Is this a diplomatic mission, or are we intending to take their technology by force?"

"Access to their warp tech is unnecessary at this point. We'd rather claim ownership if possible. That'll give us the legal rights to keep the development out of other families' hands."

"Has Ozark sent ambassadors?" a woman asked.

"Yes." Mas'ud sifted through data. "Once about ten years ago, more regularly since they developed the gate. They're treated cordially and confined to the capitol building."

Ceren said, "That's more restricted than Tsui visits."

Itzel shook her head. "Why are we so convinced the gate is functional? If we haven't seen it, and they won't talk to us..."

Mas'ud reached through Selvans and flexed his will on a blank wall of the room. People jumped. He cast a series of charts to the new screen. "Their economy took a sharp turn. Pru's system has relied on local-space trade for some essentials. Their primary source of income is hydrogen, but shipping it out is almost cost prohibitive, they're so remote."

He turned to Reza's space map and zoomed it out with a thought. "Their fuel flooded a Tsui-owned market very suddenly six years ago, dropping costs in the area. It was a galactic blip, largely unnoticed. But for Pru, their income tripled overnight. They've spread their shipments to these systems"—Mas'ud highlighted a ring of stars—"and their volume has only increased since then."

Reza crossed her arms. "They're not family owned or affiliated so they must have access to their own gate."

"And we think it's solar-powered because...?"

Mas'ud wiped his wall screen clear of economic charts and provided a fuel curve instead. "Pru isn't big enough to be shipping out this much hydrogen and maintaining open gates at the same time. Their consumption would outpace harvest."

"Maybe it's a small gate."

Kato leaned forward. "Maybe. But then why not at least partner with a family for larger territorial access? They'd have far more to gain. There's a reason they haven't picked a family. The tech for a solar gate brings in high bidders. If they want to sell, being independent is their best option. If they're trying to compete... well, they've got our attention, haven't they?"

## FARAI: *QUEENSHIP LEMPO*

FARAI FORCED her mind deeper into Queen Ningal. The Vanetta pilot was weak, they always had been, and Farai owned the queen in stronger ways even from a distance. She tore into the ship's memory and demanded information. She received the kaleidoscope view of every drone and kingship at once—the composite experience of their attack on Crane.

Farai pushed forward in time. Crane's defenses weren't an interest of hers. There were few things she knew with absolute certainty, but Crane's place in the universe was one of those.

The kings were recalled and Farai sharpened her attention. Mas'ud pushed into Ningal first. Kato followed in his wake. The two of them stumbled. Mas'ud recovered more quickly than her grandson, took in the scope of their task, and rallied to defend the ship. His organic control of structure, designing on the fly, outpaced

Crane's retaliation in seconds. But Kato seemed to be at a loss. She couldn't say she was surprised.

Only after Mas'ud warped the kings and drones back into Ningal's local space did Kato take some initiative. His strengths had always been more inclined toward war than peace.

Mas'ud displayed a stronger will by far, but he allowed Kato to play the role of hero to the rescue. Why didn't he take charge of the whole encounter? He was more than capable.

Instead, Kato took the lead, and Mas'ud followed. They sent Crane scurrying home. And with a mental flex like stretching, Mas'ud reconfigured the entire queen from front to back. Farai replayed that piece of Ningal's memory. She felt the queenship stretch and organize, deftly conforming to Mas'ud's vision. She replayed the memory again.

Mas'ud was far stronger than she expected. No one with this kind of skill could play second fiddle for very long. She withdrew from Ningal and cast her mind to Selvans. The ship greeted her with jubilance, happily sharing the latest events. And here, Farai paused. Selvans was born of Lempo. Farai had both the right and the skill to dive deeper. But she didn't have influence over Mas'ud in the same way. Of all the possible candidates for pilot on this ship, Selvans had to find the one who didn't owe her anything.

Farai extended a formal handshake, instead. She needed leverage.

# VI

KATO PULLED himself into an isolated hall in Medical. Anatomy illustrations decorated the walls: bones, the eyeball, a developing fetus. Kato eyed the last one. The door to the office he needed irised open in response to his presence. He pushed himself in. "I heard a Doctor Baird was looking for me—oh."

The doctor turned from his wall screen, two slates in one hand and a stylus in the other. It was the same doctor that had put Mas'ud down with a sedative.

"You got out."

"Yes." Doctor Baird smiled and slipped the stylus into one of his slates. "I was quite impressed with the speed at which Selvans responded to you—but then, I guess that's why she chose you."

Kato had never heard of a ship choosing a second pilot to act as a bodyguard for the first, but he found he wasn't opposed to the idea. He was better at acting than debating. "Did they have to cut you free?"

The doctor pushed across his small office to slide one of his slates into a wall slot. The other he tapped. "No. The composite retreated about twenty minutes after you left the room."

73

That was after Kato had put Mas'ud to bed. Selvans sheepishly took responsibility with a touch of her mind. Contact was muted by Mas'ud's protective raft. Kato thanked her. He floated further into the room. "Have you called me in to apologize?"

"No. I'm this ship's lead geneticist. When you were chosen as pilot we sequenced your DNA—"

"I didn't give anyone a sample."

"Selvans had one sent to our lab."

Kato poked her and growled, *You're giving away my DNA, now?*

She rolled, but Kato remained isolated from the turbulence. *It is one of my primary functions to maintain the health and safety of everyone aboard.*

*Without my permission.*

*Your well-being impacts many lives. I will maintain it based on the recommendations of your medical team.*

*Even against my wishes.*

*Are you indicating you prefer to be unwell?*

Kato captured his frustration before it could show on his face. *I want to be informed of everything regarding my health. You don't get to make these decisions.*

*I will continue to make these decisions. As my pilot you retain autonomy of mind, but I do not believe you are in possession of a biomedical degree.*

"Problem?" Doctor Baird lifted his brow. "We work directly with Selvans for a number of medical purposes—"

"I don't want to hear it," Kato snapped. He didn't need to have the argument twice. "So you have my DNA. Now what?"

The doctor handed him his slate. "We've narrowed down a list of people on board with a high propensity toward fluid psychic connection who are willing to bear your child."

Kato very slowly lifted his eyes from the names on the slate to the doctor before him. "I beg your pardon?"

"Frankly, it's easier when the pilot is a woman. We harvest eggs once or twice and manage everything else in the lab."

"You're breeding people?"

"Not just anyone." And the doctor seemed offended at the very idea. "Potential future pilots. These ships don't just pick someone at random, there's a specific skill of mind they require. Pilots have extremely flexible minds. Your brain undergoes massive alteration every time you connect."

Oh. Great. Kato wiped a hand down his face. "What happens if I don't go along with this?"

"What if you...?" The doctor floundered for a second. "I guess we would speak with pilot Mas'ud and—"

Kato's grip on the slate hardened. "No." The very notion turned his stomach. He wouldn't let them disturb idealistic Mas'ud with such an insane plan. "I'll do it, fine. But I'm not having sex with lottery winners."

"Sir, I must impress upon you—this is not a lottery—"

Kato shoved the slate into the doctor's hand. "I. Do. Not. Care." He took a deep breath. "What do you need me to do?"

"Well." Doctor Baird pulled a panel open on the wall. "Since you prefer donation, we can take a deposit today. We'll need regular additions, every two weeks or so." He handed Kato a sterile bag.

"You want me to climax into a cup."

"I have a private room you can use."

Kato clenched his jaw against the blush rising up his neck.

## Mas'ud: *Queenship Selvans*

"I was terrified, Mas'ud. Do you realize how insane this all sounds?"

He took Amala's shaking hands in his own and pressed them together. "I know, believe me, I thought I was losing my mind. One second I'm talking about ship design, and then I'm shaking hands with Farai through some mental trick."

She pulled her hands away and hugged herself. "It was so big," she whispered. And Mas'ud remembered drawing her mind out into space with him, swimming in that huge ocean. Now that he'd had some time to adjust, he found it thrilling, but that didn't mean Amala ever would. Or that she ever needed to.

He touched her shoulder. "I'm sorry I frightened you."

She shrugged, a sort of half laugh came out. "And, I mean, no offense, but you're not exactly soldier material."

Mas'ud rubbed the back of his neck. "I already tried telling them there's been a mistake. I've been informed the queens don't make mistakes." And Selvans felt that was the end of the matter. He hadn't been able to even retain the thought for very long ever since. He suspected she was redirecting him.

A blush of heat crept through his mind. From Kato. It tightened Mas'ud's stomach, and his breath shortened. Then the feeling cut off, like a door slamming shut, and Mas'ud couldn't sense his copilot without reaching further. He tried to shake it off.

On the wall slate behind Amala, their engineers' ship designs rotated. Mas'ud pushed himself closer. "I like Zola's design. It's a smart use of space."

Amala nodded. "You told her you'd try it out."

"I did. Let's do that. I have some time."

"I'll charge up the printer."

Mas'ud waved his hand. "No, no. I'll change the ship."

She bumped into the wall and dragged her hand around to find a tie-down. "You can't just change the ship."

"Why not?" He looked from her to the design. It didn't seem that complicated.

"I... you... we're moving!"

"Technically, we're not moving at all."

"We're warping—whatever! We are jumping every thirty seconds, or something."

Mas'ud smiled at her. "Amala. I'm the pilot." He stretched his hand across the ceiling and asked Selvans to stop where she was. The entire queenship settled into a lower energy state, and Selvans' androgynous voice announced: *Warp travel suspended.*

Amala's fist clenched on the tie-down until her knuckles whitened. She whispered, "Holy shit, Mas'ud."

He released the suspension. Warp in five... four... three...

"But really, the warping isn't an issue for this..." He cast a request into Selvans' depths. "There has to be a way for you to watch, doesn't there?" Selvans cleared the wall screen, and she displayed a schematic of herself. The image updated with a frame-rate too rapid for Mas'ud to discern. "Here we go, watch. First, there's these two sections here... the solid mass we carry, mostly for repairs. We'll use those as our surface area increases."

He asked Selvans to rotate and expand the image. The schematic shifted to an exploded view. "This here—"

"The warp ring," Amala said. "It has to stay round." She floated closer, holding on to the ceiling, beside him.

"Right. But it doesn't need to stay buried like this. Let's pull it out of the way..." Mas'ud dove into Selvans, sensing her as an entire whole shifting through even more vast space. He sucked the ring and all attached engine components out of the back of the ship. They maintained their connection with light latticing, dangerous in a firefight, but temporary for his purposes. Next came the fractal drone bays—larger on the outside, smaller on the inside. He drew composite crystal into a six-way helix surrounding a thicker spine.

Mas'ud shifted his focus. With the helix branches, he could deploy all drones and kings in a breath, but the warp ring was exposed from almost every angle. Tapping the mass reserve, Mas'ud fabricated interlocking plates to surround the entire helix. He added deployable fins for solar collection.

The plate rings were rotating independently. He adjusted the fin designs to avoid impacts as the plates spun. The crystal-metal hybrid flowed with his will.

That was probably enough for now, though he couldn't help chewing over the design of Selvans' gas collection vents. Something touched his arm, but the feeling was distant... Since the ship wasn't moving through local space, passive collection wasn't earning them squat. They'd have to fly slower than warp through a nebula to get any benefit.

Mas'ud heard someone call his name, and he let the vent design go for now. He didn't have a good solution, anyway.

"Mas'ud, we have a few questions for you. Mas'ud, can you hear me?" Amala held his elbow.

Engineering was stuffed full of people: Zola, Ceren, Reza, a dozen other engineers, and a few faces Selvans provided context for as Mas'ud encountered them. Most of the people held some expression of admiration or awe on their faces. How quickly had they all rushed down here?

"Mas'ud."

"Sorry, yes. Amala. You saw what I did?" She nodded.

Reza grunted. "We all watched. You put on quite a show, Pilot."

He blinked at Amala. "Do you have all these folks on speed dial? What's going on?"

She frowned at him. "You've been working for almost five hours straight. Ceren mentioned you might need to eat something, so I've been trying to pull you out."

Mas'ud pursed his lips. *Selvans, when I'm in your head, give me a sense of time.* He felt her acknowledgement through his fingertips on the ceiling. It finally occurred to him to withdraw his hand, and his connection to the ship muted slightly. His head cleared. "Someone mentioned questions?"

"Yes. Um..." An admin from the bridge raised his hand, a small slate in the other. "We're jumping quite a bit farther with every warp. Did you have something to do with that?"

"I stripped out a layer of redundancy when I moved the warp ring. Selvans knows it needs to go back in if we encounter anyone."

The admin scribbled something on his slate. An engineer raised his hand.

## NICOLAU: *OPERATIONS DECK*

NICOLAU DHAR smoothed his tie as he reviewed his background check on Jai Li. He sat back into the elevator's practical bench, prepared for acceleration. His slate glowed with text, and Nicolau scrolled through it deliberately. Jai Li's team was superb, and she herself an expert in artificial intelligence. It was that expertise that Nicolau had banked on to bring the project this far. Keeping her in a primary role should the queenship project prove viable was his first priority.

Her parents owned a small settlement on Mars, were family unaffiliated, and nothing alarming popped up in their history. Her sibling, Jai Huan, worked in an out-of-the-way corner of Europa. Had a queenship been available, Jai Huan would be on a shortlist for pilot. Their mental flexibility ranked in the top five percent.

The elevator pinged. Nicolau held onto a tie-down as the reverse thrusters accelerated. His transportation slowed, the air lock cycled, and Nicolau pushed himself onto the flight deck.

Though the area extended for meters in every direction, the entire platform was only a small part of a massive Dhar-owned Demeter drone. Pilot LaRay kept her finger on the program's progress while Nicolau managed their empire Earthside.

It was time, however, for more involved decision-making. Nicolau hooked a loop to his belt and pulled himself along a guideline that extended across the flight deck. He passed six craft in progressive states of build, each larger than a king and drastically varied in shape. They were built from crystal composite and metal alloys culled directly from Demeter, simulating as best they could the queen-birth process.

With their wiring and cavities exposed, Nicolau felt the first stirrings of doubt. He could only hope LaRay's will was enough to make Demeter cooperate with their artificial builds.

The final ship in line was physically complete though people swarmed to check every possible thing in these final hours. Nicolau paused some distance away to take it in. He allowed himself a moment of optimism. This could be the beginning of a dramatic shift in family power. If Jai Li's program worked in practice the way it worked in testing... claiming ownership of Crane's Central-Warp was just the start.

"Beautiful, isn't she?" Jai Li pulled herself along the guideline toward Nicolau and turned against her inertia to take in the view. "I can't believe we're at this point already. I'm nervous." She held her hand out. He saw it tremble. Then she noticed he was alone. "You did bring the pilot, right?"

He measured his smile to the degree of skepticism in her eyes. "Only if you're willing to mark some paperwork."

She lit up. He noticed her hands stopped shaking. "I passed your vetting, then?"

He resisted a snort. "You passed vetting weeks ago. I've been digging up AI engineers with at least half your skill to replace you if you still want to run the test flights."

She sobered and gripped the guideline. "In case the worst should happen."

Nicolau nodded. "But also in case she imprints on you during awakening. If you're her only pilot, you can't sit around the flight deck all day."

They watched the dark, angular ship for another moment. Then Jai Li turned to him with intent. "Ok. What do I need to sign?"

Nicolau handed her his slate. "This will act as an amendment to the contract you already have with us."

She scrolled through it quickly, only pausing on lines near the end. "This clause also includes my speculation on Queen Gaia?"

"The copy you gave me, yes."

"All right, let's add a line." She handed him the slate. "If anything happens to me so that I can't return to this position, being your AI engineer—" She waved her hand. "However your lawyers define that. If something happens, the treatise is released to the galactic net with my name on it. You're welcome to take credit for getting it published."

Nicolau added the clause and offered the slate for her review. Jai Li skimmed it and pressed her thumb to the bottom. Nicolau pressed his thumb beside hers. He stretched his hand to her. "Congratulations, Test Pilot Jai Li."

"Shall we get started, then?"

At his nod, Jai Li pulled herself toward the ship, and Nicolau remained at a distance. Jai Li settled somewhere inside the ship and after a moment running lights blinked on. The engines spooled. Her name pinged on Nicolau's slate. He answered the call, but no image came up.

"Can you hear me?" she asked.

"Loud and clear."

"All right." And she cleared her throat. Her next words echoed outside and, Nicolau presumed, inside the ship. "Ladies and gentlemen, please clear the area and prepare for queenship awakening."

People pushed off the ship, tugged along their guidelines, and moved some distance away. Nicolau heard Jai Li's soft breath from his slate.

"Ship is clear. AI activation in three... two... one..."

The ship powered down all at once. Lights, engine— it all went dead. Then, from the back, power rippled through the ship and everything hummed. A light popped. Nicolau held his breath. The engines spooled to a peak and held; the screaming whine reverberated across the flight deck.

Then Nicolau heard his slate speak in Jai Li's voice. *I am... awake.* The ship. The ship spoke.

Nicolau cleared his throat. "What is your name?"

*My name... is Melpomene.*

"Melpomene, you are a queenship of the Dhar family. Please do a complete self-check."

Lights blinked in sequence down the length of the ship, and Nicolau wished Jai Li's call had come with a visual feed. The self-check completed. *I am functional and self-aware.*

"Melpomene, how is your pilot?"

*My pilot is... Jai Li.*

"Yes, how is her health?"

"I'm here. I'm here. It's so big." Her voice was distant.

*My pilot is functional.*

Nicolau let out his breath and smoothed his tie even though it was clipped perfectly in place. "That's good. When you're ready, we'll start the first tests."

"Yes, I am ready."

Nicolau couldn't tell if Jai Li spoke, or her ship did.

# VII

## KATO: *QUEENSHIP SELVANS*

KATO FLOATED beside his bed and stared at the small cup in his hand. He'd done this once in a tiny space off the doctor's office, and he discovered the idea of doing it alone in his own room didn't make it less awkward. He had a cup and an obligation.

He felt Selvans warp, the smallest of tugs against his chest and hips. In a single step, they traveled half a light-year. She warped again. Again. The ship would arrive outside Pru within the hour. Three light-years later, Kato still held the cup in his hand.

Gingerly, he let the cup float beside him. He stripped and stuffed his clothes into a bin on the wall. The cup rotated.

If he let his eyes unfocus just a bit, Kato could sense Selvans calculating warp points as she marched across space. She pointed him to a room—an office—and Kato resolved an image of Mas'ud biting his lip as he concentrated. His dark hair, like a halo, filled the space around him despite his tucking it behind his ears. Kato reached out to touch. Mas'ud looked up.

And Kato remembered he was naked in his room. He jerked away, dropping his mind suddenly back into his own body. He was touching himself. Kato's cheeks

87

heated. The voyeuristic experience caught his breath. He stroked.

Then he felt Mas'ud's mind stretched toward his, a handshake. The blush expanded to Kato's chest. He couldn't touch Mas'ud's thoughts. His copilot couldn't see this. Kato gulped and covered his mouth with his free hand. What if it happened? What if Mas'ud saw him here, stretched up and gasping?

*I'd still expect dinner and a kiss good-night.*

Kato's heart slammed in his chest. He tried to back out of the handshake and tumbled. This wasn't what it looked like. He didn't jerk off to thoughts of Mas'ud in the middle of the day—

*I know.*

Mas'ud's quiet mind embraced his. Kato's panic eased. That simple statement encompassed so much. He knew. In their tangle of minds Mas'ud knew about the doctor, the donations, their need for better pilots with better minds. He understood Kato found it disturbing, that he'd tumbled into Kato's personal fantasy.

And he cradled Kato's mind, banishing the fear, filling the space with warmth. Kato grabbed the cup. He could feel Mas'ud's lips on his cheek. Warm breath on his neck. Hands—

Kato sealed the container and bagged it. Mas'ud's mind muted, as if he'd turned his attention away, and through him Kato learned they had arrived. He dressed and asked Selvans for the quickest route to Medical and then followed his copilot's heartbeat to the sit. room.

When Kato arrived, Mas'ud's smile was kind. But he knew it would be. They couldn't hide anything when Selvans blended their psyches so completely. There was no question Kato admired Mas'ud, no question the Mas'ud welcomed him in return. Only comfort.

Kato drifted lightly into Mas'ud as he took his place, and he couldn't repress the grin or the blush. Mas'ud snorted but squeezed his hand before anyone noticed their antics.

Reza brought an image of Pru up on the front wall screen. A drone passed silently across the picture. "Other than an occasional trade convoy, Pru has not had significant contact with Ozark. Don't be surprised if they're hostile to a queen showing up on their doorstep."

Mas'ud's mind muted away to somewhere outside of the room, beyond the ship. Kato focused on Reza. She continued, "We've sent an ambassador. They're still en route, but the escort drones sent back these images on approach."

She tapped the screen. A close-up image of their primary star flooded the space, filtered and falsely colored. A dark ring stood out against the field of plasma. Reza tapped the screen again. A low-resolution zoom of the ring dominated the screen. "Our estimates put the size of it at around three kings."

Kato leaned forward. "That's the warp ring? They fly into their sun?"

Itzel shoot her head. "That's the battery."

Reza pointed at it. "Which makes their warp ring four or five times this large. And if it's close to the harvest point, they must have another battery installed."

"Probably two," Mas'ud said. His mind split its focus. "That's how I'd build it, anyway. One active, one storage, one charging." Then he grunted and concentrated on the sit. room's side wall. After a moment the screen pinged. An image appeared of a man in a gray suit sitting in an office and considering their group. Mas'ud said, "This is Prime Minister Hiraka Jiro of Pru. Minister, thank you for meeting with us."

"Who is it I'm meeting with, exactly?"

Kato squeezed Mas'ud's shoulder and took over. "We are aboard Ozark Queenship Selvans. I am Pilot Kato Ozark, and this is Pilot Mas'ud Tavana. We're here to solidify our trade agreement with Pru and consider expanding it to include additional goods or services."

"Well, I'm not sure why you came out all this way. Our biggest issue is with Dhar harassing our supply paths to neighboring systems. Otherwise, Pru doesn't have anything new to offer you."

From the corner of his vision Kato saw Reza close the images on her screen. He leaned forward, "Well, that's what we're here to discuss."

## MAS'UD: *QUEENSHIP SELVANS*

WITH PRU'S Prime Minister tolerating their presence for the moment, Mas'ud brought the group's attention away from debating the solar-powered warp ring. It may have been the main reason they were here, but it didn't have to be the only one. "I think we need to investigate this harassment on their trade routes Jiro mentioned."

"I agree," Ceren said, nodding. "We need anything that'll tip in our favor."

Itzel squinted. "We can't afford to start anything with Dhar. If they are picking off trade drones, what should we do about it?"

"Announce it on the net," Ceren said. "Tattle on them."

"Would anyone care?"

Kato hummed. "They're trying to stay independent. I imagine Tsui would have something to say about it." He nodded. "I agree. We can afford the drones for recon. We don't need to engage with anyone we find."

Mas'ud added, "Dhar already knows we're here. The queenships track each other. It'd be sloppy to try taking out a Pru shipment while we're looking. Dhar doesn't want to start anything with us any more than we do with them."

"Are any Dhar queens on the way?" Reza crossed her arms.

Mas'ud reached for their vectors. "No, they haven't moved in our direction since we launched."

"Then I agree. If a family is harassing Pru, we won't find anything. If it's a pack of drifters, we can manage them and maybe get on Pru's good side. It wouldn't hurt to get a better feel for local space anyway." She nodded at Mas'ud, and he extended a mental handshake.

Between she and Kato, a track and report plan developed in the span of a heartbeat. They passed execution over to Mas'ud, and he excused himself from the sit. room.

As he tugged himself down the hall, Kato's mind reached his. *You can organize this from here, can't you?*

*Selvans has it under control already. I have an appointment to keep.*

And she did. Following Kato and Reza's outline, Selvans directed her autonomous drones like a queen bee directing her workers. The ships flooded into space, tracking common and uncommon trade routes. If they found anything at all, Mas'ud and Kato would be first to know.

In the belly of the ship, Mas'ud parked himself inside an office and cleared his throat. "Doctor, I hear Kato got a little rough with you in my Engineering Department."

Doctor Baird waved his hand, dismissing the concern. "We talked it out. No harm done."

Mas'ud floated deeper into the space. "That's good to hear. How can I help you?"

"I wanted to revisit our discussion on the legacy project. You mentioned wanting children—"

"Yes." Mas'ud smiled. "And I think surrogacy or incubation are great options. What do you need from me to get started?"

The doctor handed him a slate. "We have two solutions. You can father the children yourself. We have selected a list of people on board who are willing. Or, we can collect a regular deposit of sperm for artif—"

Mas'ud laughed and pressed the slate back into Doctor Baird's hands. "Let me stop you right there. I transitioned at fourteen and had a hysterectomy at twenty. You won't be getting any sperm donations from me."

The doctor blinked. "Oh." Then his face lit up. "Oh, that's brilliant!"

Enthusiasm wasn't the usual response. "What?"

"This is perfect. Mas'ud, did you have your ovaries removed entirely, or just your uterus?" Then he looked down at the tablet, still speaking. "It's OK if they were, we can harvest spinal stem cells for cultivation. This is great."

"I still have them."

"Fantastic!" The doctor's grin bordered on manic. "With Kato's sperm and your eggs we'll be able to cross the bloodlines of two pilots for the first time. Since you both were chosen to pilot, it's highly likely your children will inherit the same mental flexibility."

Mas'ud found his thoughts circling close to Kato, and he closed his mind quickly. "You want Kato and me to have a kid?"

"Oh, a dozen at least." And he passed the tablet back.

A grid of toddlers grinned up at him, each a different outcome of the Mas'ud/Kato genetic lottery. Mas'ud touched the screen and felt his chest tighten. He blinked a little faster. They were doing this so backward. Kids before kisses? Mas'ud let out a breath of a laugh and nodded, eyes a little wet. The toddlers laughed back. "Yeah, OK. What do I do?"

"Today? Just a shot."

With his head full of kids and his shoulder a little sore, Mas'ud pushed himself out of the doctor's office without a clear destination in mind. In the middle of the hall, Selvans demanded his focus. Mas'ud dropped into the senses of a distant drone in space that was following the path of a trade route. Ahead of him, a Dhar kingship dropped out of a warphole into local space.

## LaRay: Queenship Demeter

LaRay MOVED her pawn to intimidate Demeter into giving up the chase but was doubtful it would work.

After decades of play she had yet to defeat her own queen. She was starting to suspect the ship was cheating. Perhaps Demeter had a chess master aboard that she was consulting.

Her negotiations with Maylin were frustrating, and the game was supposed to satisfy. Instead, both were letting her down. LaRay scowled at Maylin's image on her screen. "Dhar won't be made a puppet to control your peace. If Tsui isn't going to stand in and demand the return of stolen goods, then what are you standing for?"

It infuriated LaRay that Maylin's expression didn't change. She continued, "It's an open secret that Dhar claims ownership over half the independent systems in this quarter, including Seorus. We won't take a side in your family scuffle. Don't offend me by claiming it's anything else."

LaRay scowled. "We gave Paomia aid without being asked. It's time you repaid that favor."

Maylin hung up on her.

And LaRay refused to admit she might have deserved that. Demeter took her pawn and last bishop in the next three moves. She gritted her teeth and threw her mind across space instead. Out of her ship, beyond the system, she touched and greeted Queen Melpomene.

Demeter resisted the connection. It wasn't natural. LaRay overruled her.

Queen Melpomene reported her location and status. Her small army of drones, led by only six kings, moved through space in an ever-widening net. The ship drifted through the raw gas and metals of a nebula. She collected the materials with the help of two large-mouthed collector-class drones. She finished production on a seventh king and immediately cast it into space.

Except for her pilot, Melpomene functioned entirely without crew. She was much smaller than any other queen in flight, and LaRay appreciated her nimble and far-reaching warp ability. Without a full crew's worth of mass to move, Melpomene could warp clear across the spiral arm in two jumps, a distance Demeter would take two weeks to cover.

Her queen grumbled at the comparison: Melpomene wasn't a true queen. Just a composite with impressive AI. The pilot couldn't accept a proper handshake.

LaRay dismissed her ship's irritation. Melpomene was the only thing going right today. She reset the chessboard.

# VIII

## KATO: *QUEENSHIP SELVANS*

KATO FLOATED in the pilot's chair, mind and body one with Selvans. He watched the unidentified king through Selvans' drone, which was some distance away. The king hadn't moved since appearing abruptly into local space, so Kato kept his drone stationary as well. It was unclear to him if this was a standoff or some kind of mistake.

He pinged the king, seeking information—to whom it belonged, first, but why it was here, as well. Had they come across a family ship stalking Pru's trade routes? It was such a foolish move. A confrontation would force Ozark's hand.

The ship pinged back as Dhar but provided no queen. Kato didn't know what to make of that. Every ship berthed at a queen.

Seven unidentified drones dropped into local space forming an oblique ring around the king. Offense-capable drones. Fighters. They held their positions and distance.

Disturbed, Kato redirected a handful of Selvans' scouts to the area and called on another handful of fighters to take a stand. He pinged the strange fighters for identification. They returned Dhar. No queen.

What kind of ships had no queen? Selvans rolled. Artificial ones. She didn't like this situation, and neither did Kato. His fighters arrived, and he arrayed them in a defensive grid.

The no-queen king didn't move.

## MAS'UD: *QUEENSHIP SELVANS*

Mas'ud dropped his concerned turmoil into Selvans. Who were these ships from? What did they want? Why this wild-west standoff in the middle of empty space?

In the week since the king had first arrived, three dozen drones and two more kings dropped into local space. Their offensive power grew with each passing day. Selvans met it with drones of her own, willing to defend but not about to make the first move.

But today six more no-queen fighters showed up, and Kato finally sent out Ozark King Aplite with a full complement of armed fighters to bolster their side in the no-man's-land debate.

Aplite was a good choice. Selvans, and therefore Mas'ud, knew the pilot had a history of resolving tangles rather than conflating them. She could negotiate in a pinch.

But none of this resolved the situation at hand, and Mas'ud tore through Selvans' extensive library of staff and genetic memories for any sign that this had happened before or any clues on what to do about it. His latest mental handshake faded with time, and he renewed it with an irritated push in the mystery king's direction. Every ship had a queen.

Selvans tried to soothe his manic tear through her knowledge. *The answers are in that ship, not within me.*

*Then talk to it!* Selvans made a recoiling gesture that spoke of a horror, and Mas'ud jerked his attention to her. *What's wrong?*

*I can't speak to it. It's not a real king.*

Mas'ud didn't follow. *You make contact with Crane scouts all the time. They're just AI.*

*You do not understand. Listen.* And Selvans took him deep into her mind. He dove down into brightness—a crushing light. The whining spool of her engines hummed like a rapid heartbeat, a massive understanding of sound and power that wiped out his ability to think. But then, as he adjusted to the light and noise, he understood everything here to be massive flows of data. Visual, electrical, magnetic—the heart of Selvans was a supercomputer.

*Listen.* She reminded him.

Mas'ud listened. There was too much at first. Everything Selvans knew and sensed in any moment flowed through this place in live streams. There were rivers of data from the drones and bigger rivers from kings. Smaller streams of data flowed from each person on board in contact with Selvans.

She guided him deeper. Where the data flowed faster. Where Selvans' ocean churned hardest. Ten indistinct flows circled inside. Their edges overlapped and blended, and some were so close they flowed together. Mas'ud resisted Selvans' push. He didn't need to go any closer to sense the minds here. These were Selvans' connection to the ten other queens in the galaxy. Connected to her deepest self. Like family.

And if he concentrated, Mas'ud could trace knowledge of drones and kings back to one of these ten streams. Every ship had a queen. Every queen knew its mother. Every ship was a distant sibling of every other. Selvans herself was an almost identical clone of Lempo—their bond was strongest.

These Dhar ships in the middle of empty space weren't just artificial constructs. In the only sense Selvans could connect with them, he knew they hadn't been born—they'd been created.

There might be a queen. Mas'ud lunged upward, out of Selvans' deepest space. He passed through the bright core and further up into surface understanding where he could reach for Kato. There might be a queen for these ships that Selvans couldn't sense because they weren't part of the family. Dhar could have built a new queen from scratch, and these drones were that queen's army.

## PATLI: *KINGSHIP SCORIA*

THIS WAS nuts. Kingship pilot Patli McLaren slammed her fist on the console's composite membrane and found the impact on the forgiving material insufficiently loud. Typical. She couldn't even vent her frustration. With a mental yank she launched Scoria into space and burned thrusters at full blast toward the new drone. Queenship Kishar fell rapidly behind. It was a waste of propulsion mass, and she'd probably be written up for it, but Patli didn't care. She had no other way to express her distaste for this assignment

The drone came up quick. Patli flooded her forward thrusters to cancel her momentum. She came to a delicate stop only a few feet away. "Connect up, already." Patli released her control on her kingship. Scoria could handle alignment and tethering on her own.

While the ship maneuvered—far more delicately than Patli had—she leaned back in thought and groaned. What had possessed her to mouth off? Morta knew, she *knew*, that Patli could handle the harder salvage runs. Why had her sister lined her up for another three weeks of repair work? It wasn't as if they were short on people to patch up Kishar from her latest gas and mineral harvesting mission. Yet here Patli was, escorting a bloated drone into the sun because some engineer decided they'd make a good solar-powered bomb or something.

Scoria's connection locked. Patli boosted them both toward an array slowly expanding at her upper one o'clock. Beyond fetch and return, she hadn't paid much attention to her task at hand, but as the array came into view, she tapped into Scoria's database. What was going on here?

Scoria's information was short. The grid of drones would act like a giant solar cell, charging up a battery drone for unprecedented levels of mobile power. The design had been purchased through a trade agreement with some outer system. Patli wasn't surprised. McLaren wasn't known for innovation with Dhar directing their every move.

Ok, sure. Patli eased their velocity as they approached. She could be pissed about the assignment, but screwing it up with a collision would make her entire year something to regret. Most of the drones here were little more than paper-thin composite, linked to each other and absorbing radiation. Patli was hauling the battery.

She manipulated her view, identified the gap in the pattern where her drone belonged, and turned control back over to Scoria. The kingship maneuvered with short, precise bursts of her thrusters. When in place, she prompted the drone to connect. Scoria disengaged. Battery and solar cells merged together, connecting wire-like composite crystal from one to the other under Queen Kishar's direction.

Patli watched until Scoria's drift brought the queen back into view. She cruised back to the ship with less force. She deserved the shit assignment for mouthing off. Patli wasn't utterly without remorse. But if Morta didn't hand her some more challenging work, she might just go looking to Dhar. At least they had regular contact with other families, even if it was all skirmishing and pissing contests.

# IX

KATO DRIFTED in his quarters, unable to drag his mind from Selvans. He envied Mas'ud's easy way of protecting himself from her. She worried. Fretted. The anxiety was unfamiliar to Kato and didn't seem normal for a queenship. But then, artificial queenships weren't normal, either.

Their standoff in empty space continued. After weeks of cautious buildup Kato was almost prepared to send Selvans herself in to wipe the board clean. He could resolve simulations that played out over the course of months in a couple of hours. It strung him up—this living through the waiting, the tension growing as their forces built up in a line. He wasn't prepared for doing nothing.

He considered reaching out to his grandmother; she was only a thought away. But what did that say about his ability to pilot that he'd run to her at the first sign of a Dhar ship? The king- and drones-with-no-queen hadn't made even a slight move toward them. They weren't even at war with Dhar at the moment!

And with Selvans running herself in circles with worry, Kato hadn't found a chance to breathe in days.

She rolled his mind with every repeat of her concerns. Kato was drowning.

He held a cup with a membrane lid in his hand and tried to remember what it was for. Every time he blinked, Kato saw a flash of Selvans' thoughts. It made concentration impossible. How did Mas'ud block her out?

Kato felt him at the door a moment before the knock echoed in the room. Kato pulled the composite membrane open with a thought, and Mas'ud pushed himself into the space. He didn't look around.

His warm hand met Kato's palm. Then there was silence.

Kato blinked. His hand shook a little. He took a deep breath and found Selvans circling in her worry behind a distant wall. He let all his air out in a rush and rubbed his forehead with the back of his other hand. "Thank you."

Mas'ud took the cup from his hand and let it drift in the air beside them. "Better?"

Kato leaned closer. He tilted Mas'ud's chin up with a single knuckle. The man's wide, dark eyes welcomed him. His mind was a warm, safe space. Kato kissed him. Just a touch of lips.

It was Mas'ud who pulled Kato closer with a hand on the back of his neck. Mas'ud who opened first and offered. Kato squeezed his hand and gave in. Their knees bumped.

Kato remembered what the cup was for.

Before he could shy away, Mas'ud's warm hand slid across Kato's stomach, up his chest. They let the shirt drift. Their thoughts mingled, and Kato's worry faded. Mas'ud knew. When Kato slid his belt free, Mas'ud was there to unzip his pants. He slid them down. And Kato laughed, a soft huff. He felt Mas'ud's curiosity. Kato cradled his cheek. "Why do we wear belts in space?"

Mas'ud snorted and kicked Kato's pants off his feet. Kato missed the feel of his breath. He tugged Mas'ud close for a meandering kiss. Then Mas'ud arched against him, hands fisting in Kato's short hair. Kato read his need. He gripped Mas'ud's hips close, cradled his ass with soft palms and hard fingers. Mas'ud thrust against him. Their hips and bellies interlocked like a puzzle, soft places meeting hard points. And Mas'ud's desire spiraled up, dragging Kato with it. Their breath came in sync.

Kato bumped into the wall. Their kiss broke. Mas'ud immediately grabbed a couple tie-downs, pinning Kato in place with his own body. He smiled and whispered, "Get naked."

A flutter of ideas transferred between them. Kato's heart raced. He yanked his underwear off and stalled. Too many possibilities. Mas'ud laughed, and the sound delighted Kato. He watched the shake travel up Mas'ud's chest and rattle his shoulders, fascinated with the way it threw his head back. That needed to happen again.

Mas'ud put his palm on Kato's chest and dragged it down. Their skin was dark on darker, two different shades of night meeting at a single point. Kato touched Mas'ud's hand with his own at the bottom. His head dropped to the wall, full of Mas'ud's smile and sparks of heat. He groaned. And with their thoughts so tangled together, Mas'ud read his need, blinking in neon. Kato dropped into Mas'ud's mind and lost all sense of himself.

Kato came back into his own head to the sound of a crinkling bag. And Mas'ud was there instantly, his warm hands on Kato's, his eyes soft. Kato pulled him in, growling low. He swapped their positions and devoured Mas'ud's lips until the man whined against him.

Their thoughts fell over each other. Kato whispered, "Show me what you want?" It came in a cascade, and Kato returned it with suggestions. Their ideas went back and forth until Mas'ud panted against the wall and desire fractured his organized thoughts.

Kato got to work.

## Mas'ud: Queenship Selvans

Mas'ud traced patterns of swirls on Kato's shoulder, comfortable in their warm tangle. Kato drifted in and out of sleep. He burrowed against Mas'ud's chest and held tight. Mas'ud let him dream until he muttered something.

"What was that?"

Kato propped his chin up on Mas'ud's shoulder. "Said, I wonder if these children I'm making are ever going to meet me."

"Of course they will. I want to be really involved in raising our kids."

Kato pulled back a little to eye him. "Our? What?"

"I donated eggs weeks ago."

"But they said..." Mas'ud felt him dismiss that thought. "We have a kid?"

"Probably several."

Kato huffed and burrowed close again. When Mas'ud wondered if he'd drifted off again, Kato muttered, "I really owe you dinner."

Mas'ud laughed and stroked his hair. They remained tangled, half asleep, for some time.

A thought from Selvans rapped hard against Mas'ud's mental wall. He cast his attention into her tumultuous ocean and saw the nonqueen battalion at a distance. Two more kings had dropped into local space and aligned themselves with the offensive grid. Mas'ud didn't know what to make of it.

If a family was intending on making some kind of assault, this wasn't the way to go about it. And Dhar didn't string out their waiting like this. They attacked a target suddenly, with all force at their command. This build up over weeks, with additional ships coming hours and hours apart—it was weird.

Mas'ud pushed himself closer. Selvans resisted, but it was past time they learned more. Mas'ud didn't extend a mental handshake. He pressed right up against the void where a queen's mind should have been. It flexed. Mas'ud plunged an arrow of thought straight into the weak spot.

Space shattered.

## JAI LI: *MELPOMENE*

JAI LI GASPED awake, full of pain and brightness. She found herself screaming, but the sound was only hoarse croaks, as if she'd already been shrieking for hours or days. She couldn't make sense of herself. There was no up or upright. The space around her extended forever in every direction. Actual space. Vacuum.

Something pressed on her mind, and she shoved back without any sense of moderation. She punched through the brightness and lost herself again in the sheer volume of sensory information. Light, sound, radiation from every direction, thoughts from a thousand small points, waves of direction from a large source. She rebelled and gasped for air.

Several of the small thought points belonged to her. She reached for them, hoping to find something familiar.

Hoping to find some balance in the chaotic everything. She felt herself move without taking a step. Her understanding of the space around her shifted, like turning the page in a book. The thought points were here now, right here, and she couldn't understand them.

But they faced off against two dozen other thought points, and Jai Li understood a threat. She lunged forward, extending herself in all the ways she knew how. Once the threat was gone she could make sense of herself.

# X

KATO JERKED against Mas'ud in the confining sleeping bag. Selvans slammed him with data, and even half asleep, he understood the urgency. He pulled on Ceren and Reza. *Get up. Sit. room, now.* What time was it, anyway? It didn't matter.

Beside him, Mas'ud whispered, "Oh, shit."

Kato saw the battlefield in slow motion. The unclaimed Dhar kings and drones couldn't hide their source anymore. An oddly built queen had dropped into local space just above them and released her entire army. It wasn't big. Selvans had more mass to work with, but nothing about this encounter made any sense.

Why attack family ships in the middle of empty space? Why the slow buildup? What was this abrupt assault supposed to gain? Kato scattered Selvans' drones to confuse the enemy and buy time. He needed to get to the cockpit.

Mas'ud hauled himself out of the bag first. Kato followed right behind him. They pulled on the bare minimum of clothing in silence. Concern and alarm sparked between their thoughts. Then Mas'ud closed himself off from Kato, and he was left only with Selvans' rioting emotion.

"What's our next step?" Mas'ud clung to a tie-down on the ceiling, his knuckles white.

Still floating, Kato shoved his shirt down into his pants. "Now you call Dhar and ask them what the hell is going on. We should also let Farai know."

"Great." Mas'ud jerked himself out of the room. Kato followed.

The pilot seat flowered open; soft layers of petals exposed a dark red core. As he settled into the membranous chair, Kato floated away from himself. The edges of his body blurred with the edges of Selvans until he couldn't easily tell them apart. He felt Mas'ud like a distant heartbeat, steady—a fixed point in the ebb and swell of Selvans' thoughts. With that anchor to orient him, Kato dove into strategy.

His primary concern was to buy time. This queen and her army claimed to come from Dhar, but until Mas'ud could gather information, Selvans insisted she couldn't verify it. In retrospect, they should have called on LaRay, or at least one of her daughters, when the first drone acted oddly.

In space, Kato instructed his kings in a series of avoid-and-harass maneuvers. The drones he manipulated as a single cloud; they spiraled and cut between pairs of ships, tempting crossfire.

The Dhar drones reacted far faster than Kato expected. Selvans crunched numbers and displayed an alarming statistic. The Dhar ship attacks were one hundred percent accurate. There was no deviation.

Kato pulled his ships close to their kings. The drones shunted their power to shields and clustered for defense. Dhar drones circled them.

Then, an enemy drone powered its thrusters to full and slammed into a cluster of Kato's ships. Its mass splintered three of his drones, and the Dhar ship was utterly destroyed. Suicide. Kato pulled on the pieces, but he didn't have Mas'ud's skill with formation.

Another Dhar drone impacted his ships. A king rocked. Kato received an instantaneous damage report and estimated casualties.

But no word from Mas'ud.

The time had come for more impressive firepower. Kato pushed Selvans. The queenship warped and released her full complement of fighters. A plague of drones descended toward the Dhar queen in helixes. They shot to destroy.

Selvans' estimation of the Dhar queen's mass blinked in alarm. It was growing. Then, an entire unit of ten Ozark drones and their commanding king shut down. They tumbled in space, rapidly exiting the immediate area, taking their human crew with them.

## Mas'ud: Queenship Selvans

MAS'UD REVIEWED Kato's understanding of the fight, and through him both Farai and LaRay gained the knowledge. His divided mind hosted each queenship pilot separately. Farai provided context and strategy for his negotiation with LaRay, and it was working.

LaRay's connection with him faltered; her distress echoed through the link without any attempt to hide it. This unnamed queen belonged to her, but an assault on Ozark, on any family, was not part of her instruction.

And now the queen appeared to be in rebellion.

*She won't let me near.* LaRay insisted. *I can't meet her mind. We're already en route.* Then a burst of feeling: restraint/mercy/pacifism. She didn't want the queen destroyed.

Selvans provided an estimated time until Demeter's arrival. Mas'ud didn't like the number. *We will defend our crew and assets, LaRay. You have assaulted us. Don't ask for leniency.*

*This is a mistake, an error in her code. It can be corrected.*

Mas'ud thrust his thoughts at her. *And in the interim our people will die. How many crew do you have aboard the queen and kings?*

LaRay's thoughts stalled, a hasty wall went up between them. Mas'ud had no time for this. He lunged through the weak barrier and pulled the information from her own memories. One pilot. No crew. The entire queen had been constructed in a hanger.

In a sudden sweep, Selvans lost a unit of fighters and their king. All contact with them simply ceased. Mas'ud tried to pull the crystal composite they were made of back toward Selvans. He couldn't touch them. The material had been severed from Selvans, killed. External sensors identified the crafts as they drifted away, the status of the crew aboard unknown.

Farai grabbed his attention. *There's a pilot in that queen. Talk to her.*

Yes. There was a single crewmember. She had to have influence. With Mas'ud's help, they could bring the rogue AI under control.

Mas'ud dropped his connection to LaRay and Farai, heaving instead toward the Dhar queen. He crashed into a wall built like nothing he'd ever felt before. Static and noise. More information than signal.

*MY NAME IS MELPOMENE.*

The voice hit like a meteor, and Mas'ud staggered under the weight.

Another unit of drones and their king died.

Mas'ud scrambled to right himself. The ship shouted again, backwards and upside down. He barely recognized the phrase. *ƎNƎWOԀ˥ƎW WⱯ I.* She scrambled the letters and shouted them—righted everything except the E's and shouted again. Noise.

Mas'ud grabbed a phrase, and she yanked his mind open. Through him she invaded Selvans. His queenship shuddered as she started to die. Selvans began rapid evacuation. Crew and officers first. She ejected Kato into an unmarked pod, cutting him abruptly out of her mind. Mas'ud was next.

He resisted. Through sheer force of will Mas'ud maintained his connection and threw himself at Melpomene. The oblique attack just drew her attention, and she tore him out of Selvans herself.

Mas'ud went blind with pain.

## LaRay: Queenship Demeter

Demeter warped onto the scene. For a moment, LaRay couldn't make sense of the chaos. Then Jai Li pulled her army back, and the charred husk that was formerly Selvans became clear. The debris cloud expanded. This was far beyond rogue. Jai Li couldn't be reasoned with. It fell to LaRay to stop her.

She encouraged Demeter to release the drones. All of them. She felt a full quarter of Demeter's mass take flight.

Jai Li warped away. Her destination wasn't immediately clear. For the first time, LaRay cursed the artificial queen's independence. When Demeter finally located Melpomene, her first few warps seemed arbitrary, but they resolved into a straight vector. Demeter followed the line directly back to Earth.

LaRay shoved her handshake at Farai. The pilot resisted her greeting. *Why can't I hear my grandson?*

LaRay shouted, *Melpomene is on a direct path to Earth. Selvans is destroyed. Defend yourself!*

LaRay was readying Demeter to follow the artificial ship when several SOS pings hit her awareness. Then several more. Selvans might be dead, but her crew had been evacuated. LaRay redirected her drones.

There was no easy way to clean up this mess. Dhar would suffer for decades, the consequences of killing an Ozark queen outside of a declared war. Recovering their people was the least she could do.

Her drones began returning with survivors. Demeter identified each one as they arrived, shuttling people to Medical or down to housing as appropriate. Thousands of people, the vast majority of them alert, terrified, and distrustful.

Demeter identified Pilot Mas'ud Tavana. He lay unconscious in his escape pod, battered and scratched from his rough evacuation. LaRay had him brought to Medical, but as he was transferred she extended a tentative mental handshake.

Mas'ud had no barriers to keep her out. His mind fluttered, torn and traumatized, and he reactively flinched at her delicate touch. LaRay asked for his memory of the attack, but all she saw were flashes of light and an intense pain. She searched deeper, looking for anything that could help her understand why Jai Li had turned against her.

But much of Mas'ud's memory was simply gone. Torn from him entirely. As his body was submerged into a tank of oxygenated fluid in Demeter's medical bay, an artificial mental wall pushed LaRay out. Demeter would protect his mind as well as his body. LaRay let the ship care for him.

*Scan the wreckage for Kato,* she asked. Her ship did so, locating the smoking remains of the cockpit and identifying an ejection point. She calculated Selvans' drift and spin and estimated a possible cone of space where the pilot's evacuation pod could have been ejected. LaRay sent a swarm of drones along the expanding path. They discovered three different pods.

Kato floated, semiconscious, inside one of them. He struggled weakly against the crew that pulled him out, muttering nothing that made sense. His mental walls remained in place, though he seemed confused; LaRay was rebuffed twice and then welcomed with no apparent logic.

She dove into Kato's familiar mind, but his understanding of the fight was as fractured as Mas'ud's. He lacked any memory of his time as a pilot, and his recollection of his training up to that point was spotty at best. LaRay traveled even further back, deeper than she had cared to go with Mas'ud. Kato had a more important history with Ozark, and LaRay needed to know...

Aside from a few moments of sharp clarity, Kato's mind struggled to piece his memory back into a correct order. It wasn't utterly missing, as with Mas'ud, but the soup it had become was worse.

Or better. LaRay halted the crew before they submerged Kato in the medical bay. Before Demeter's automatic walls could kick her out. She pulled pieces of Kato's mind together, untangling bits here and reforming pieces there. She recognized huge swaths of his history. Pieces of strategy she'd taught, herself. She could rebuild them. Mas'ud's cause was lost—there was nothing there to fix—but Kato she could save.

His work on this chessboard wasn't done.

## XI

## KATO: *QUEENSHIP DEMETER*

KATO GRIPPED the edge of a tank. He was floating, but it was a suspension different from microgravity. His fingers slipped. Something pulsed along his arm. Kato tried again, thrust his arm up, pushed through a resisting layer, and gripped the edge of a tank. His strength faded quickly. The tank throbbed. The fluid suspending him sucked and drained away. He coughed, ejecting more fluid in a sudden full-bodied spasm. Air stung his lungs, and he exhausted himself in moments.

Hands reached in for him. They pulled his arms and shoulders, sat him upright. Kato pushed them off and tangled in tubing. He swiped at his eyes and blinked through the bright light. He was connected to something: the back of his wrists, his head, his spine. As soon as he became aware of the connections, they disengaged. Small filaments pulled out of his skin as they retreated. He rubbed the tiny red dots they left behind.

"How are you feeling?"

Kato looked up. A doctor in white held her hand out in case he needed it. Her smile was practiced. Calm. Professional. He shook his head.

"Are you in any pain?"

What had happened? Kato looked at the red dots on the back of his hand, watched the last of the blue liquid suck out of his... It wasn't really a tank. More like a pod folded into the wall. Another pod was full, beside him. A man with shoulder-length black hair was suspended inside.

"I need you to follow my finger, please."

Kato snapped his eyes front at her tone. He followed her finger. Left, right, up, down. He blinked into her penlight and accepted a swab in his mouth. He'd been through this before, a long time ago. He found the practiced motions familiar.

She produced a slate. "What is your name?"

"Kato Dhar."

"Your birthday?"

"January fourth, ninety-seven fifty-nine."

"Your rank?"

"...I..." His rank. He had a military rank, of course. Name, rank, serial number. He stared at the bars on the doctor's shirt, stitched into place. He could name her rank... but he didn't know his own. He looked down and discovered he was naked, which made sense. He was in the medical bay. In critical life-support. Something catastrophic had happened.

"Your rank?" she repeated.

"I don't know."

The doctor nodded. "It'll come back to you." She quizzed him on a number of things. Some he could answer, others he couldn't. The older facts were easier—school, training, hobbies. But the newer ones: direct reports, his own boss, the nature of his mission and its outcome... Kato just shook his head. She didn't seem perturbed in the least.

Kato repressed his anxiety. Would his memory be blank forever? Did anyone know what had happened? Who else had been with him?

The pod beside him flowered open. The man inside didn't react. Blue fluid was sucked away, and the compression made him cough.

"Was he with me?"

The doctor pushed herself over to her new patient. "No. He's an engineer. There was an accident."

Kato took her word for it. He wasn't an engineer. That didn't feel right. But he was something...

Who was Kato Dhar?

## Mas'ud: *Queenship Demeter*

MAS'UD COUGHED to clear his lungs and spat oxygen-rich suspension gel from between his teeth. The ship's pod pulsed around him, wakening his limbs from their lingering stupor. The room was absolutely dark. He wanted a shower—a proper earth-side shower with water and shampoo.

A hand touched his shoulder. Mas'ud jerked in surprise. He turned his head but the darkness persisted. "Who's there?"

"I'm a doctor. Are you in any pain?"

Doctors didn't work in the dark. Mas'ud blinked hard. He touched his hand to his eyes and found them intact. "I can't see."

"Yes, that was a concern."

Mas'ud heard her fingers tap on a slate and cocked his head. The pod hummed with familiar energy. He traced the edges of his space. The thin, flowering membrane curled around his fingers. It told him calm/peace/heal. He pushed his thoughts back. *What happened to me?* It didn't respond.

The doctor hummed. "Can you tell me your name and date of birth?"

"Mas'ud Tavana. March twelve, ninety-seven fifty-five."

"And what is the last thing you remember?"

Mas'ud turned inward and immediately found yawning gaps. He could replay a series of painful flashes of light, and he knew static. Loud static. But between the noise was blank nothing. He rubbed his arms and shook with a sudden case of cold.

"Mas'ud?"

He whispered, "I'm an engineer from Earth. I graduated..." He was on a ship. He'd always wanted to work on a queenship. "I must have a degree."

"You have two," the doctor said. "Do you remember what your project was?"

But there was only an echo of empty space. "What day is it?"

"July seventeenth, ninety-seven eighty-six. It's Tuesday."

Mas'ud shook his head. He didn't have any orientation in this year. He had no memory at all except flashes and pain. Violence. "I can't remember."

And he couldn't see.

The doctor told him to wait where he was. Told him she'd help in a moment. He heard her assisting someone to his left out of a similar pod. They spoke in quiet voices that receded across the room.

When the doctor returned she helped him out of the pod and guided his hand to a tie-down on the ceiling. He gripped it while she toweled him clean and then helped him dress. The clothing was unfamiliar. It did nothing to orient him. He fingered the over-starched shirt cuffs.

"There are a few things you need to be aware of, Mas'ud." He turned toward the sound of her voice. "You were recovered in an escape pod. Your body sustained heavy trauma; several broken bones, torn muscle, a puncture in your lower gut. We managed to repair the majority of the physical damage. Your ovaries and tubes were removed. We've adjusted your testosterone regimen as a result."

Mas'ud's breath left him in a rush, a sudden punch to the gut he wasn't prepared to take. Anger boiled up inside him, hot and sharp like glass.

"You also sustained rather severe head trauma. A substantial portion of your visual cortex is... well... for lack of a better term, it's torn. There are several such tears throughout your brain that have likely contributed to your memory loss. You've made a recovery nothing short of miraculous regardless of the damage."

He couldn't breathe. "Will my memory return?"

"Bear in mind that you've been in suspension for only a few weeks—"

"Doctor." Mas'ud narrowed his eyes despite being unable to see. "In your professional opinion, will my memory or sight return?"

"No." She took a breath, and Mas'ud put his hand up to forestall her.

"What can you do for me in the meantime?"

The doctor turned—by the distance of her voice—and there came the sound of a membrane irising open. "Let me introduce you to Kaia Mockta. She's an engineering intern. She's volunteered to help you adjust for the next few weeks. She knows how to get in contact with me should you need anything."

"Kaia," Mas'ud said and stretched on his hand. She took it, small and firm.

"Mas'ud, it's nice to meet you."

"Did we not work together?"

"No, but I am a fan of your work."

Mas'ud gave a tight smile and wished he knew what kind of work he'd done.

## ESHA: CENTRAL-WARP STATION

ESHA RECEIVED a ping on her slate from a rather small Dhar drone. Their serial number had an odd syntax, but they forwarded payment soon after. She processed the payment and called the drone. "You guys are a little small to be collecting anything, aren't you?"

Static returned to her on the radio. Esha frowned and tapped her connection, resetting it. Only static.

The payment cleared, and she shrugged. If they wanted to waste a round trip on visiting dignitaries, then that was their issue. She cleared the drone for warp.

Esha's office flooded with blue light as the ring activated. The tiny drone pushed itself through. The warp ring sucked closed. Her office plunged back into darkness.

An Ozark drone pinged next in line. While she was processing their payment, she received clearance for a returning Dhar drone. Esha opened the warp gate. Her office glowed blue.

The tiny Dhar drone with the odd serial number came back through. Now what was the point in that? As the gate closed, energy pulsed between the small drone and the gate ring. It leapt around the circle, frying a box of resistors, and then dissipated into space. An error flashed on her slate.

"Dammit," Esha muttered. She called the drone. "You guys OK in there?" But only static echoed back at her. Her display showed the Dhar drone continuing its flight away. She huffed and conference called the entire line of drones waiting for transport. "Hang tight, guys, we arced. I'm sending someone out on a walk right now. Give us a half hour."

A chorus of resignation returned to her. After paging a mechanic, Esha checked the video from a camera perched outside her window. She watched the small ship return and slowed playback when the arc washed out her camera. The video was useless but her readouts showed some kind of magnetic field crashing into her ring. That wasn't right.

Esha called her boss. "Mx. Crane? I think I have something you'll want to review."

# XII

## KATO: *QUEENSHIP DEMETER*

THEY KEPT calling it retrograde amnesia. Kato braced and pressed a pneumatic bar away from his chest. The machine offered resistance. He knew big things: how to walk and talk, how to play chess. But the details of his family service escaped him. He pressed the bar, concentrating on the muscles in his back that ached and protested but needed to be worked. His body man leaned against a machine beside him, available for questions at all times of the day. Kato didn't mind the babysitting. He needed the help.

He didn't seem to have trouble making new memories. Kato had the image of a dark-skinned, black-haired man in the suspension pod beside him fixed in his mind. It came back to him at odd moments. But anything before the attack on his kingship, before even earning the status of kingship pilot, was just a wash of nothing.

Kato released the pneumatic bar and changed position to work his legs. He pressed, and the machine adjusted for greater resistance. They said he'd get his memory back with time. That it would be faster if he were exposed to familiar things he'd forgotten. But his ship and his crew had been destroyed. He didn't recognize his room or the smattering of possessions in it. He

131

couldn't quite navigate the ship without a map on his slate. If his memory were going to come back, he'd need to see someone more familiar than the man behind the lunch counter.

He released the bar and braced on the wall to change his position again. The queenship's thoughts sparked over his fingertips: protection/anticipation/a depth of potential. It didn't appear that anyone else could hear her, but Kato found the occasional overlap of her thoughts comforting, so he didn't mention it. Perhaps it was due to his position as a kingship pilot. Pilots had to be more sensitive to that kind of thing.

From the front of the training room a woman barked, "Pilot on deck!"

Everyone in the room shifted. Kato found himself moving automatically. He disengaged from the resistance machine and floated in open air, orienting himself in the same direction as the pilot. He braced one hand on a tie-down to remain stable.

She drifted regally into the room. Her nearly black skin stood out against the metallic Dhar family colors: brass and gold. He found her pilot suit familiar. It wrapped around her skin as if it had been painted there, and Kato recalled a sense-memory of the way it could stretch as he moved. He fixated, digging hard for more. But the memory faded, and he lost its edge.

"Kingship Pilot Kato." She addressed him directly.

Kato stiffened at attention. "Ma'a—" He broke off the word, immediately sensing it was incorrect. She didn't frown, not quite, but Kato knew that look. He ventured, "Miss..." When she didn't correct him he gained confidence. "Miss LaRay."

She assessed him up and down, a quick jaunt from head to toes. "I'm happy to see you've returned to fitness training so quickly. The loss of your kingship and crew is a setback we won't recover from lightly, but I'm confident you'll be flying for me again in short order. Your skill is invaluable to this family."

"Yes, Miss LaRay. I look forward to it."

She nodded and turned away, bending her head toward an aid as she went. As the pilot exited the room, people returned to their routines, and Kato turned back to his. But some thought pulled at him. He asked his body man, "That woman. Who is she?"

"Pilot LaRay, leader of the Dhar family and our commanding officer."

He knew that. And the ease with which he responded to her command felt real to him. But there was a deeper familiarity he couldn't shake. "But who is she to me?"

"Sir—" The man's pause made Kato look up at him. "—Sir, she's your mother."

Kato felt the room darken around the edges as his focus narrowed to his body man. It would explain quite a bit—how he was skilled enough to pilot a kingship, how he could speak with the queen they were on... Kato brushed his fingers against the wall, and the ship acknowledged him: kin/descendant/future.

## MAS'UD: *QUEENSHIP DEMETER*

KAIA MOCKTA turned out to be invaluable to Mas'ud's sudden shift in lifestyle. "My sister lost her eyesight," she explained. "Macular degeneration. But she was only thirty. The docs think the microgravity had something to do with it. Anyway, they eventually squeezed her in for replacements but we had an interesting six months of figuring out how to manage until then."

She taught him simple ways to cope that seemed obvious in retrospect: Everything had a place in his room and that was the only place they belonged—his laundry was put away in the same drawers—allowing him to memorize the layout of the space rapidly. The ship knew he was blind and automatically ensured his food was provided in the same layout. Kaia taught him the basics of braille, and while his slate still responded to vocal commands, he could now interact with it in a quieter manner. He even received a small earpiece that synced with his slate, allowing him to listen privately instead of broadcasting his browsing habits.

And while he was thankful for her help and rapidly adjusting, he felt removed from anything of greater significance. He couldn't remember moving onto the queenship, though Kaia assured him his engineering work here had been impressive. None of his supposed colleagues had contacted him since he was released from Medical. And even though he'd been excused from work for another two months pending a checkup, Mas'ud craved something to do.

And he didn't quite accept the story of his accident, either. There was nothing overtly wrong with it, that he could tell, but it didn't sit right, either. He cradled his slate in one hand, perched in a corner of his chambers, and listened to the recorded timeline again.

- **13:00** – Engineering team launches from Demeter.
- **14:50** – Rendezvous with Queenship Melpomene. First reports of instability upon contact.
- **15:03** – Melpomene grants engineering access. It's determined that Pilot Jai Li is not in control of her ship.
- **15:05** – Engineering reports resistance from the queenship regarding access to ship design and records.
- **15:20** – Melpomene grants engineering team leader Tavana access to flight records. Negotiations over ship design begin. Melpomene confirmed unstable, refuses to recognize fealty to Demeter or Pilot LaRay.
- **15:45** – Engineering team leader Tavana granted access to adjust ship design.
- **15:50** – Support engineering staff jettisoned.
- **15:55** – Pilot confirmed dead.
- **16:00** – Melpomene attempts to jettison team leader Tavana. Tavana designs an escape pod and survives. Unconscious, severely injured.

- **16:00** – Queenship Melpomene classified rogue.
- **19:24** – Team leader Tavana recovered by Demeter.

The record provided him with a list of his apparently handpicked team. He read through their personnel files and didn't recognize them. Demeter herself provided the timeline, the official record of events as she experienced via drone. There was no better source.

But Mas'ud had never considered fieldwork before, and the special assignment feel of the mission struck far beyond his interests. It maybe wasn't out of the question if Pilot LaRay herself requested his assistance, but Mas'ud couldn't see himself acting like a knight-in-shining-armor.

Aside from this vague sense of friction, however, Mas'ud couldn't rightly say the story was wrong. He had no memory at all to guide him either way. Just a gaping sense of loss in his head and another in his chest. The one was his memories, and the other, he figured, was the complete hysterectomy. Having kids someday had been a dream of his, but there always seemed to be plenty of time later.

So he bit his tongue about the failed mission and about the rogue queen, and he let Kaia guide him around like a cheerful Labrador each day.

## Patli: *Kingship Scoria*

McLaren Kingship Scoria burned her port thrusters for two seconds. It was a small nudge, made smaller by the massive drone attached to her nose. With this much charged material, Patli couldn't afford a big swinging mistake. She assessed distances by wire—her forward screen was flooded with light, the view was useless. The drone held so much power it glowed as brightly as the sun that powered it.

Patli tapped her starboard thrusters. Then tapped them again, slowing her glacial movement down to continental drift.

At the perpendicular, the drone extended a coupling, reaching out to an array of likewise charged and delicate drones. Together, the group formed a triad. The coupling connected and locked. Patli instructed Scoria to disengage. The drones pulled themselves into a tight format, weaving cables of crystal composite between them to spread the load.

Patli pinged Queenship Kishar. The power drone was complete.

She drifted some distance away, admiring her work. Morta was right to select her for this assignment. Building McLaren's first mobile warp ring? It would put her name in the historical memory of every queenship in the galaxy. Right next to that independent system who sold them the tech. Paliu or Prew or something. She hadn't read the whole file. Apparently the battery prototype nearly bankrupted the family, but Patli figured it was worth it if Dhar couldn't dictate their actions anymore.

McLaren, growing into its own, and here she was building the future. The first space station pinged Patli, and she directed Scoria to connect with the long structure. Alongside her kingship, Patli guided each station into place, one by one in a ring large enough to rival Kishar's girth. Each station, built from linked drones, wove themselves into their neighbor with power cables and transfer locks—growing with queenship instructions.

It took hours. Patli relished every minute. Queenship Kishar provided regular monitoring of the crew in each station as she linked them together into a single ring. The last piece came from a specialized drone built into the ring opposite the triple-drone battery. Patli didn't read the debrief on its purpose—a stabilizer of some kind. She just needed its orientation.

Kishar recalled Kingship Scoria as the last drone locked into place. Patli watched the new warp ring come to life as her ship maneuvered home. A blue ocean rippled into existence, casting eerie light into space. A collector-class drone headed for the ring.

# XIII

IT DIDN'T take long for Kato to grow bored with resistance training and chess matches. He demanded more information: about his former kingship, about his crew, about more familiar places and people. Yet, his memory still remained stubbornly blank.

There were rare flashes of emotion or a sensation that knocked him over with its strength—but they were fleeting and left him more frustrated than ever.

He quickly outgrew the need for a body man and took his concerns directly to the pilot. After all, wasn't he her son? She promised him a new crew.

At four in the morning, a knock sounded on his door. Kato checked the tie on his pants and touched the membrane to iris it open. On the other side floated a striking man with a wicked grin and a buzz-cut of blond hair. "I hear you're in the mood to pilot again." He held a folded cloth.

Kato took it. A Dhar pilot suit. His pilot suit.

"Get dressed, flyboy."

Kato tapped the membrane of his doorway, and as it irised closed he heard the man laugh. The sound was hearty. The bare edge of a memory teased him: laughter and yearning. Kato got dressed. When he opened the

139

door again the man stuck out his hand. "I'm Syaoran, your new second. Let's go!"

A brief handshake, and then Kato had to catch up. Syaoran chatted as they moved through the corridors. "I figure we can jump into a king on downtime and see what it jiggles loose in your head. Regs need at least four folks in a king for live combat, but for just a loop around local space, I can be your backup. Do you remember what Demeter looks like from the outside? All angles and bronze. I heard they anodized half the ship, but I don't think they can do that to living crystals..."

In the hanger, Syaoran guided him with a flourish to a particular ship. "Ah, Kingship Marl. Not the brightest crayon, but she'll orbit when you need her to. I think Mama Ray is cooking you up a new one once you've got a crew settled."

"I don't have any history I can remember with the officers here."

"Don't stress it." Syaoran pulled himself into the king-ship and urged Kato toward the big, central seat. "I can yank a few hotshots out of their day jobs for you to meet."

"Any good engineers?" Kato touched his fingertips to the composite metal, and the ship brightened with lights.

Syaoran stretched his body out, hands behind his head. "Now what do you need an engineer for? They're all holed up in their offices. Not great for live-action adventure, you know?"

Kato looked up at him. "It just seems like it would be handy to have one hanging around."

"I'll look into it. Now stop chatting and get us powered up."

Kato rolled his eyes and settled further into the chair. A mental touch, like a handshake, came from the kingship. Connecting was familiar. Right. He belonged here.

Syaoran made himself comfortable in the copilot seat and guided Kato out into open space.

## MAS'UD: QUEENSHIP DEMETER

KAIA TURNED on the big drafting slate in Engineering and called up the CAD program. "You don't have to be here, you know." Her voice drifted away from him.

Mas'ud knew she wasn't trying to be insensitive. He couldn't put into words the urge he felt to do something—some means of design. Shadowing her work, even if he couldn't see it, allowed him a little closer.

He navigated the perimeter of the room and discovered an additional desk. Kaia snorted. "If they ever decide I'm worth wasting an intern on, that's where they'll work." Mas'ud drifted his hands over the magnetized table. He located a drafting slate, turned it on.

It occurred to him that all of his design work had only ever been visual. He knew the shapes and principles, but the slate didn't provide three-dimensional access. Mas'ud drifted his fingertips over the surface. Verbal cues dictated into his earpiece a basic but functional system. He found the CAD program.

His years at university allowed him some layout familiarity with the system. Mas'ud started a new project, just a simple cube, and hovered his fingers over the shape. The slate couldn't provide tactile feedback, but his earpiece dictated dimensions and coordinates on a z-axis. With some concentration he could build a mental picture.

Mas'ud slowly manipulated the blank cube into a simple twisting lattice structure. It wasn't anything fancy: a basic project for students unfamiliar with the program. But without visual assistance for rendering, Mas'ud built the shape by working the math and co-ordinates. His recall was rusty. How long had it been since he graduated? Had he ever really designed this way before?

"Hey," Kaia said, just before her hand touched his shoulder. "Not bad for a blind guy."

"It wouldn't pass any tests, I'm sure."

"Still. How did you do it?"

He tapped the earpiece. "The slate's reading coordinate points to me. I input the equations."

She snorted, "You happen to know the math for helical line?"

"I guesstimated."

"No wonder they had you leading a team. I don't think they even teach the numbers anymore. It's all visual interface." She pushed away from him, back to her desk.

Mas'ud didn't feel accomplished. There was no sense of familiarity in this room or these big slates. He didn't even miss the design work he must have been doing. There was just... nothing. And how was he supposed to build something new out of that?

So he could bullshit his way across a CAD program—He wouldn't be passing even a basic intern test without a better way to interface.

And was it even something he wanted anymore? Had the accident and his memory loss changed him? Mas'ud couldn't find passion within himself, and it was hard to say why. He was still recovering from a traumatic experience. How much of what he felt, or didn't feel, was just body and mind chaos lingering from that day?

Mas'ud closed the CAD program and shut off the slate. He felt certain of nothing.

### FARAI: *QUEENSHIP LEMPO*

FARAI SLOWLY pieced together a better picture. A news broadcast here, a passing mention there. LaRay's panic echoed in her head. *Melpomene is on a direct path to Earth. Selvans is destroyed. Defend yourself!* And since then, all efforts to reach her simply fell into black space.

The echoing emptiness in Lempo where Selvans used to be, the smaller spaces where Mas'ud and Kato used to be, haunted her. The queenship was a devastating loss, not to mention the full million-and-a-half crew. Her grandson. All wiped out in a moment of chaos that LaRay hadn't explained.

But Dhar couldn't hide every mention of Melpomene on the open net. For weeks, Farai chased rumors and ghosts. Now she had evidence. And leverage. She could provide a strong case to any Tsui mediator if that's what it came down to.

A broadband SOS shrieked across Lempo's awareness. Farai unfolded the information package immediately. Crane had called for backup at the Central-Warp Station. An unknown enemy was destroying their fleet and refused to communicate.

Farai's chest constricted. Too many of Mx. Crane's details matched the buildup Selvans had observed just prior to the assault on her. Melpomene was on the move.

Farai cast her mind out to the far reaches of space, tapping into even the most far-flung Ozark drones and kings. *Return home*, she commanded them.

Over one million individual ships turned toward Earth.

## XIV

## KATO: *KINGSHIP SCHIST*

KATO SMILED to cover his embarrassment as Syaoran exaggerated the story of his ship's destruction to comical proportions. No one would believe him. But if the enraptured faces were any judge, no one was going to call him on the half truths. Kato's smile froze a bit at the edges. Other than a debriefing report from the ship, how would he know what was truth?

Syaoran leaned into him, wrapping an arm around his waist. Kato broke out of his introspection before it could get maudlin. "And Prince Dhar, over here with his perfect hair, just saunters into an escape pod—No big deal, right? Survives a homicidal AI, practically dead from the trauma, and two days after critical, Mama Ray finds him in the gym." Syaoran tugged on Kato's ear. "I'm telling you, he's like a cat or something. Nine lives."

The cadets around them laughed. Kato swatted Syaoran's hand away. His second pushed out of range and called to the younger crowd. "Aye. My kingship pilot's gotta finish eating, so scram." He helped the soldiers abandon the mess and came floating back with uncharacteristic silence. Syaoran settled in the space in

145

front of and above Kato, inverted. He fiddled with a water bulb he hadn't drunk yet.

"Do you have to call me that?" Kato poked at the tofu mash he was supposed to eat. "Prince Dhar, I mean."

"It's your family title."

Kato made a face. "I'm a kingship pilot."

Syaoran snorted. "We have fifty of those. I could be one in a pinch." Kato wasn't anybody's prince, but Syaoran wouldn't let it go. "We even have, like, three princesses, but we have exactly one Prince of Dhar. People need to remember that!"

"What for? Demeter already birthed a queen this century, and my sister Iesha is the pilot"—a sister he only remembered in childhood flashes too old to rely on—"so I'm not in line for anything."

Syaoran's water bulb bounced off of Kato's head. He looked up to find his second pinning him with a narrow-eyed gaze. "What's Ozark's total defense force in Earth's local space?"

His answer was automatic. "Two hundred thousand ships. Give or take?"

Syaoran caught his water bulb. "If we take over Central-Warp, what's the first thing we should do?"

"Shut it down and starve out the other families, gain control of the hydrogen market and, by association, space travel." Kato frowned. Where was this coming from?

Syaoran reached for him. "If I do this…" His hand slipped around Kato's wrist.

Kato lunged upward, tangling Syaoran's long limbs to catch him against the ceiling. Kato gripped the tie-downs, his breath suddenly quick.

Syaoran's wicked smile flashed. "You are a soldier, Kato. You're the Prince of Dhar. You have more knowledge, will, and political power than everyone on this ship except Mama Ray. You can do anything."

Kato gripped Syaoran's shirt. Syaoran's breath hitched. Their eyes locked, and for a single blinding second, Kato felt his body come alive. But Syaoran's hair wasn't long enough, and his skin wasn't dark enough. Kato's vision flashed to the man in the submersion tank. Who was he? Kato's fist tightened. He released Syaoran and looked away. "You're here to build my kingship team. I want an engineer. Stop admiring my ivory tower and get to it."

Syaoran leaned into him, his voice a whisper. "Yes, my prince."

## Mas'ud: *Queenship Demeter*

THE VACANT spaces inside him were growing. Mas'ud stared at nothing—Kaia, or a wall, it didn't matter—and he saw nothing. The gaps in his memory never seemed to knit any closer together, and while she tried to hide it, he sensed the doctor was worried.

His aborted attempt at design didn't encourage him. Wandering aimlessly around the ship just left him even more lost than before. And Kaia tried to cheer him up, but Mas'ud wasn't just sad, he was incomplete.

He dragged his fingertips on the ceiling. It was comforting to touch the metal-crystal hybrid. A queenship was never cold, more like body temperature. Living metal. Aware.

But even with that powerful being watching over him, Mas'ud knew something critical was missing. Yes, his memory, his heart, and his knowledge of everything for the past several years weren't just blocked or fractured—they were gone. But there was something more that left a gaping hole he couldn't identify.

He oriented against the ceiling, holding tightly to a tie-down so he could press his cheek to the warm composite crystal. The therapist his doctor had ordered wanted him to start making new memories, make new friends, but Mas'ud couldn't just ignore the gaps. They weren't foggy. They were missing entirely.

The doctor told him last week that pieces of his brain were missing. His visual cortex was almost entirely gone, arbitrary sections of gray matter just... absent. But according to records, he hadn't arrived with severe head trauma, there had been no cracks in the skull or detectable blunt force impacts. No explanation.

Mas'ud tightened his grip on the tie-down and squeezed his eyes shut. He couldn't help but wonder who or what was playing with him. Something had taken pieces of him, his sight, his memory, his... Mas'ud forced his hand away from his belly and back into the throbbing composite crystal.

He didn't know what he wanted anymore. He sought completeness in a way he couldn't properly define.

He slammed his fist against the living metal and felt it flex under his will. Just another skill he couldn't manipulate anymore. Mas'ud yelled at the ship, a wordless scream of despair. He reached outward and into the queen.

She responded. Mas'ud choked as Demeter met his mind, enfolded him, cradled him. This was impossible. His awareness of self expanded. He heard the ship flex, felt the corridors like veins, touched every mind onboard.

This. This was the void in his head. This was missing. Then Demeter kicked him back into his own limited body.

Mas'ud yanked his hand and cheek away from the metal-crystal composite. His breath shook. He wept.

## OOLJEE: *QUEENSHIP NINGAL*

OOLJEE ZAH cast their attention across space, as far as Vanetta Queenship Ningal's sensors could stretch. They sought any information on Crane Central-Warp.

Since the SOS, no instruction had come from Ozark, and Crane seemed to be silent, too.

The distances twisted, and Ooljee had to pull back. They still couldn't hold an understanding of vast spaces, and Ningal only helped so much. Ooljee suspected other queens assisted their pilots in more powerful ways. But they had Ningal, and it was more power at their fingertips than ever before, so they'd manage.

Ningal drifted at subwarp speed through a nebula, collecting raw gasses and minerals. It was slow going, but without any Ozark direction, they had all the time in the world.

And Ooljee had enough time as Ningal's pilot to wonder just how in control Ozark really was. Had the previous pilot caved under threats? Family hostages?

Ooljee stretched their mind inward, touching the crew of the queenship, seeking. They needed help. People with experience and skill, people who knew the families and were willing to advise them. So far, the search had only turned up Ryung. The man was friendly enough, competent in both battle strategy and theory, but he'd never served, never flown, and was as wet behind the ears as Ooljee. They needed professionals and they were starting to think Ningal had a significant lack of talent at her disposal.

Suddenly, an Ozark command rang through her mind. Ningal turned in space and calculated a jump.

She warped, warped again, and warped a third time before Ooljee could stop her. They slammed their mind into the queenship, demanding attention. Ningal stalled. So that was how Ozark ensured compliance. They simply commanded, and Ningal obeyed.

*Am I your pilot?* they asked.

Ningal responded, *Yes.*

*Then you will do as I say. Do not accept direction from anyone else.*

*Acknowledgement.* Then a ping. *Queenship Lempo demands our return to defend Earth.*

*What are we defending Earth from?*

*There was a moment of nothing.* Then: *Unknown.*

*Is this the same unknown that attacked Crane?*

*Unknown.*

Ooljee resisted the urge to ask what the ship did know. They already knew she responded poorly to sarcasm. *What is the exact agreement signed between Ozark and Vanetta?*

The ship downloaded the document into their brain, a single swipe of information that made them shudder. Taking it all in at once was not a smooth process. But it was effective. *Our debt to Ozark cannot ever be repaid in this manner. The years accrue faster.*

*Affirmative.*

*How long has Vanetta been bound to Ozark?*

*Sixty years.*

Ooljee squeezed a fist. It was time to move on. Ningal, *bring us to Crane Central-Warp.*

*Queenship Lempo demands our return to defend Earth.*

Ooljee threw their mind against the queen and forced her to reorient toward Central-Warp. *Crane sent us a broad-spectrum SOS first. We are honor-bound to assist them.*

*Affirmative.* Ningal warped toward Crane. In moments long-range sensors picked up the dwindling swarm of fighters holding against unidentifiable attack drones.

Ooljee mentally reached for Ryung. They shared the situation as it unfolded through X-ray and gamma ray sensors. Ooljee expressed their thoughts on assisting but emphasized protecting the queen. Ryung offered a distant approach and then two more related options.

Ooljee tried to keep their connection with Ryung while executing the first design. When Ningal stopped traveling a few light-years from Central-Warp, they released the ship's entire complement of drones and kings. The army warped the final distance without Ningal and engaged the mystery enemy on sight.

Crane pinged Ningal. Ooljee had to drop Ryung to accept the connection. It came through on visual. A wide-eyed woman was speaking a bit breathlessly. "Ozark, if you're gunning for a better price by letting us wallow this long, I'll have you know it's under control, and I will personally erase your credits from this database, so help me—" Her eyes flicked to the side. Her hand darted up to touch the screen. She issued new attack orders.

Ooljee cleared their throat. "I'm not here from the Ozark."

The Crane woman flicked her eyes briefly back. "Explain."

Ooljee took a deep breath and felt Ningal's membrane flex around her. "I am Ooljee... of Vanetta. And I am here to answer your SOS."

The woman blinked. Her mouth worked for a second and then snapped shut—she had nothing to say to that.

"I'm sorry," Ooljee said, filling the silence, "I'm unfamiliar with any protocols surrounding this kind of thing. I've been dropped in without any guidance. Do you still require assistance?"

"Yes." The Crane woman wiped a hand down her face. "God, yes. Thank you."

"It's all right." Ooljee urged, wishing they could reach out to comfort her. They pushed Ningal to warp. The queenship complied, appearing suddenly in Crane's local space. With queenship firepower suppressing the enemy, Crane and Ningal fighters could finally turn the battle. Ooljee tracked unknown drones abandoning the area as they warped away. With some luck, they wouldn't be back.

"I'm Esha."

"Ooljee Zah. It is nice to meet you."

"Zah? You're Ningal's pilot, aren't you?"

"Yes, I was just selected."

Esha's voice softened, "Then you should take the name Vanetta. It's yours by right."

Ooljee queried Ningal and the queenship confirmed the name was now theirs if they wanted it. Ooljee wasn't sure. They cleared their throat, and got back to the matter at hand. "I have a proposal—"

Esha held up her hand. "I'm not actually authorized for much of anything when we're in a state of war. You'll want to talk with Mx. Crane."

"Very well."

Esha transferred the call.

## XV

## KATO: *KINGSHIP SCHIST*

KATO SMILED at his assembled team and passed drink bulbs around. Syaoran had come through with a team of five more—yes, even an engineer—that Kato knew instinctively he could lead to victory. They had the experience, the attitude, and most importantly, they lacked Syaoran's odd hero-worship of Kato's position in the Dhar family. At least, so far.

Chu'si cackled at some joke echoing around the group, her short, pixie crop of red hair styled into severe spikes to the left as intimidating as Syaoran's wicked grin. She was aggressive in and out of the navigation seat. But when quiet Dania touched her arm for attention, Chu'si reined herself in immediately.

Dania's critique of the group's latest flight training bloomed over her slate, and she stretched the tablet to the center of the table for everyone to see. Una leaned in and blocked everyone's view. "All right, an eight out of ten. We're getting better." She stretched up and out of the way, "So what's our trouble spot?"

Kato sucked on his drink bulb. Dania's voice, as quiet as her touch, held the group entranced. Except for Syaoran. The man drifted into Kato and their elbows bumped. "Hey, have you heard back about the king?"

"It should be ready tomorrow." Kato leaned close so their conversation wouldn't disturb the others.

Syaoran snorted softly. "I can't believe you talked Mama Ray into building a custom one for us."

"Hey, you suggested I stop hiding from my family title. What good is it for, otherwise?"

"You know, the usual." Syaoran made a dismissive gesture. "Intimidation, blackmail—"

Kato chuckled. "Do you ever default to anything that does some good?"

"What, like getting laid?" Syaoran waggled his eyebrows.

Kato rolled his eyes. "Does that really do good?"

Syaoran smacked Kato's shoulder. "It does me!" Then he grabbed Kato's arm and laughed, more words spilling fast.

Kato didn't hear them. The hand on his arm was hot like a brand with tight, flexing, individual fingers digging their nails. He saw a crown of black hair and the dark skin of a man he knew. His lover arched against him, breath paused for a gasp. Kato flushed.

"Hey." Dania's voice broke into the vision, and her tone morphed into something more severe. "Something you kids want to share with the class?" She was taller.

"Yeah," Kato said, not entirely sure that was the right answer. Then the memory faded, and Dania was... back to being Dania: brown curly hair, bright amber eyes, and the shortest one in the group. "No." Kato corrected and shook his head. He pulled away from Syaoran's confusing touch. "No, sorry, continue?" He ignored the sharp glance Syaoran sent his way and pushed away the lingering mental whiplash. Mixed memories gave him a headache. Kato squeezed his eyes shut for a moment. He couldn't trust what he saw.

He had a ship, a crew, and a family. Whatever ghosts were locked away in his head could stay there.

## MAS'UD: *QUEENSHIP DEMETER*

MAS'UD WAS nothing more than a bundle of wired nerves. He twitched and flinched from everything. His heart raced. His muscles jumped. He couldn't calm down. It'd been days.

Days since Demeter had reached out to his mind and held him close. Days since he'd experienced the nearest thing to being whole since waking up in that suspension pod filled with goo and plugged in like a power outlet.

Kaia touched his hand—he twitched away—and then she grabbed his wrist and pressed a sandwich into it. "You've got to eat. We're not leaving until you do."

Mas'ud took a large bite. Leaving was a good motivator. The chorus of voices in the mess left him disoriented and frazzled. Kaia was running out of ways to convince him to socialize as Mas'ud fell deeper into depression or insanity—he wasn't sure which.

He'd mentioned, only once, that Demeter had touched him. She had dragged him immediately to the doctor and he had fallen asleep to the oddly familiar sensation of being drugged. Mas'ud knew to keep his mouth shut now, but keeping it all inside without any way to reconnect was tearing him apart. The voids were growing. Mas'ud didn't know how to stop them.

He shoved another bite of sandwich into his mouth, and the chewing allowed him to focus externally for just a moment. Kaia was laughing. He heard at least two other voices, maybe three. They didn't speak to him. They didn't talk about him. Mas'ud simply wasn't there. He groped for something to drink, and Kaia guided the water bulb to his hand, but she didn't try to engage him in conversation.

Abruptly, Mas'ud found himself irritated. He clenched his jaw and let go of the sandwich. "Tell me everything you know about the accident."

The laughter around him died in a sour break. There was an offended pause. Then Kaia said, too sweetly, "You've already read the entire report from Demeter."

"I'm not interested in the report. I want to hear what you know. Or my colleagues. Or my supervisor—I have one, don't I?"

"Of course—"

"Why haven't I spoken with them?"

"Mas'ud, you're on medical leave," Kaia said shortly.

"For how long?"

"Until your memory comes back, or until the doctor clears you for work."

Mas'ud balled his fists. His memory wasn't coming back, and with his "the spaceship is talking to me" episode, he'd never be cleared. He huffed and forced his hands to relax. Something bumped his chest softly. The sandwich, maybe. No one removed it for him. "Please take me back to my room." He couldn't reliably find his way around without someone guiding him, and the additional dependency rankled.

"You haven't eaten."

"I'll order something from the room."

She sighed, but excused herself quietly. A soft chorus of good-byes grated against Mas'ud's guilt string. He wrestled it into his anger. He hadn't asked for this. He didn't ask for her. Something was wrong. The queenship refused to touch him again, and the doctor was two opinions away from calling him crazy. He couldn't keep going on like this.

Kaia left him in his quarters without a good-bye. That was fine by Mas'ud. He touched his way slowly around the room until he came to his tablet set into the wall. He removed it and asked the ship's database a question he hadn't thought of before.

*Was anything from the rogue ship salvaged?*

*Affirmative.*

*Where is it being held?*

Interior ship coordinates were dictated directly to his earpiece. Mas'ud's grip strengthened. He needed a guide.

## WINONA: *KINGSHIP FELSITE*

WINONA TSUI checked her king's vector out of boredom and asked for a status report on each junction of her transport. The ship returned the same velocity and direction she'd been staring at for a month. Junction statuses reported in order from the kingship all the way down to the tail drone. Seventy linked drones in a long row, stuffed with processed hydrogen, nearly all of them without crew. Winona's transport team consisted of a mere seven people scattered about the rig, isolated by space for the duration of their voyage.

She pushed away from the console, but the only place to go was the conjoined bedroom/pantry, and she soon paced back to the pilot seat. Soothing classical music filled her small space, and she refreshed the news for the seventh time in a few minutes.

One of her team members, Devraj, challenged her to a virtual game of pong. It distracted her for nearly an hour. But then she was still in the pilot chair of her king, transporting a standard load of hydrogen from Crane Central-Warp to AC-C on her way to Earth. Only seven more weeks to go...

Winona slid her finger across a slate in her console. Vector line, temperature readings, gas percentages in their local space, two dozen Ozark drones on long-range sensors, a pulsar from oblique three o'clock helping locate her in space—*wait.*

She slid back to the long-range sensors. The number had increased. Nearly three dozen Ozark drones were marked passing at a distance. All of them headed for AC-C. At both full sublight speed and warp frequency. She watched their ping markers march up to her transport and beyond, a hundred more following like a swarm of insects.

"Hey, uh, Winona. You seeing this?" Devraj crackled over the speaker with heavy disbelief in his voice.

"Yeah... I don't get it? They're not transport drones."

"Are they all headed for AC-C warp station?"

"That's what the vectors say. But I don't have anything on the news, and nothing has come from Maylin." The pings passed her transport and kept going, covering her distance in a fraction of the time. "There has to be something going on."

"That's a big waste of fuel. Should we tell Maylin?"

"Can't hurt. I'll call Qu Yuan."

"Let me know."

Winona spread her palm against Kingship Felsite's composite membrane and reached. The Tsui queenship accepted Winona's mental handshake and passed her to Maylin.

The queenship pilot greeted her, *May you be at peace.*

*And you as well.* Winona settled into her sister's confident security and let the details of her knowledge pass between them.

Maylin's silence held intent. *This is unprecedented,* she said, revealing her own additional details. Ozark ships from every stretch of the galaxy had turned toward home—as far as Maylin could tell, every single one.

*What is going on?*

*I don't know. We are expending a large chunk of our resources to rebuild on Paomia. Farai has not reached out to me. It may be time that I speak with her.*

*Are Ozark warring with Dhar?*

*Not officially, but family disputes have never prompted them to consolidate at Earth before.*

Winona rubbed her forehead and sighed. *Keep me in the loop?*

*I will. Stay at peace.*

*You as well.* Winona pinged her crew for attention. "Gentlemen, we're picking up the pace. Disengage drone seventy and bring it to the front."

Devraj acknowledged, and asked, "Does Maylin know what's going on?"

"No. And it makes me nervous. Let's get ourselves back to civilization ASAP." Winona gazed at the Ozark ships on her long-range sensors and felt her stomach drop.

## XVI

## KATO: *KINGSHIP SCHIST*

KATO STRETCHED his mind through the kingship, visualizing the path they needed to take between asteroids. Kingship Schist converted his thoughts to a plot and asked for verification. Kato verified. Without further direction the ship maneuvered.

Syaoran asked, "We're picking up the power ring, right? They don't want the crystal structure, too?"

"According to the salvage order, just the power ring," Dania said. "Demeter's been warping at a good clip for quite a while now. I'll bet they don't want us wasting the time."

"What's the rush?" But Syaoran just muttered the question and sighed.

Chu'si whistled. "Hey, my drone scans are coming back. You'll want to see this."

Kato flexed his mind and called the information to the screen before him. An oddly built kingship was orbiting anti-spinward. "Whose is it?"

"Drones can't identify. There's major damage to the rear composite structure. I wonder if the warp ring was compromised?" Kato sensed her pulling the drones around for another pass below the ship.

"Why would we salvage a damaged warp ring?" Eleuia asked.

"Don't know," Dania said. "Una?"

The engineer was quiet for a long time. As images and sensor data from the drones continued to flow in, they ventured, "This ring isn't built like anything I've ever studied in action before."

Kato grunted. "What about theory?"

"Well, there's something... Chu'si, can I get a scan from directly behind?"

King Schist burned port thrusters to cruise around a large asteroid, and the unidentifiable kingship came into her visual field.

And Una hummed. "Kato, I believe this is a prototype ship. The warp ring conforms closely to a theoretical model published a few months ago. There are some changes, and the ship itself was built without a crew in mind. There's no life support or even a pilot's chair. I recommend complete salvage."

Chu'si snorted. "A prototype ship with no queen, no family, drifting damaged and abandoned in a random system with no habitable or mine-worthy planets. No one was supposed to find this. How did Demeter know it was here?"

Eleuia laughed. "How do the queens know anything?"

Dania suggested, "Maybe Gaia told her."

"Gaia is dead." Una's voice held conviction.

"We don't know that for sure," Eleuia said. "The queens could be in contact—"

"And they just haven't mentioned it to anyone for thousands of years?"

"Enough. No theological debates on my ship." Kato nudged Schist around to the rear end of the odd king. "Una, let Chu'si know where it's safe to cut this ring free without damaging anything important."

"The whole ship is important."

"The warp ring is more important than the whole. The order says we're here for the ring, so that's what we're taking."

They huffed but began notating a diagram for salvage.

## MAS'UD: QUEENSHIP DEMETER

MAS'UD FOLLOWED a suspended line through the huge open space of Demeter's repair bay. In his ear, an AI patiently guided him. He hoped it was bringing him to whatever wreckage of his accident they had salvaged, but if he was honest there wasn't any way to tell, really.

With the tiff they'd had, Kaia wouldn't be back to check on him until morning, which meant he had more than a few hours to get himself entirely lost. He intended to take full advantage.

His entrance to the repair bay had been a bit fraught. It was a bottleneck of traffic, and without sight, he'd been jostled and bumped around while he tried to locate the main guideline. From there, traffic had only decreased until now. He took another fork to the right and had yet to encounter any person for several minutes at least.

The work of repairs echoed and bounced across the bay, but they were very distant and getting farther away. The AI informed him that this section housed obsolete projects or was just open space. It was probably packed full during wartime, but with Demeter en route somewhere, the majority of the bay stood vacant.

*In thirty meters, turn left.* The AI's voice spoke in a generic, soothing tone. Mas'ud let his palm trail along the line. His fingers bumped a junction. He pulled himself left. *In ten meters you will reach your destination.*

Mas'ud put his free hand out in front of him. He found a piece of crystal composite, damaged—possibly burned—but definitely a ship. With the utmost care, Mas'ud pulled himself around the craft, getting a feel for the shape and form of it. It was larger than he expected. He asked his AI, "What is this vehicle?"

*You are in contact with Kingship Gneiss of Queenship Selvans of Queenship Lempo.*

"Lempo belongs to the Ozark."

*Accurate.*

Something wasn't adding up. "What was the name of the queenship my engineering team attempted to salvage?"

There was an odd delay from the AI. *Queenship Selvans.*

No. Mas'ud didn't remember the accident, but he'd read and re-read that debriefing report. "Who is the pilot of Queenship Selvans?"

Another delay. *She has been destroyed. There is no pilot assigned to Selvans.*

Basic AI didn't delay before answering. They had array access to all of their data, allowing instantaneous results. Someone, somewhere, was lying to him. He pressed the button outside his earpiece to turn it off. He didn't know who to suspect: Kaia, the doctor, or Queenship Demeter herself. Maybe all three.

Mas'ud pulled himself around the kingship until he located an entrance. Severe mass-impact damage had torn a gaping hole in one side, revealing the interior. He shuffled through the tear and explored the pilot chair by touch. If luck was on his side, enough energy still sat in this ship to give him a few more clues. Who was Queenship Selvans, for one, and if he was attempting to salvage her, why cover it up?

His earpiece crackled despite having been turned off. The AI stated, *Engineer Mas'ud. Your presence is requested on the bridge.* Mas'ud resisted the urge to snort. Sure it was. He fished his earpiece out and tucked it into a pocket.

The pilot's chair molded to him—a reactive motion to the pressure of his body. In the same manner as when he had connected briefly with Demeter, Mas'ud reached his mind out to the kingship around him. He asked for help.

The ship responded with far more than information. Mas'ud sank deeply into the pilot's chair. A full array of sensory data flooded his system. The ship self-checked and sacrificed a portion of its mass to seal the pilot's cockpit from the vacuum of space.

Without Mas'ud's input, the ship broke its moorings and zipped rapidly out of Demeter's repair bay. Only then did a very familiar androgynous voice connect with his mental handshake. *Queenship Pilot Mas'ud Tavana, I have found you*. The voice carried relief/connection/joy/grief along with it, and one of the gaping holes in Mas'ud's mind was filled by a presence far larger than his own.

## JAI HUAN: *OPERATIONS DECK*

JAI HUAN floated impatiently in a plain, small Dhar drone. They'd located him in an isolated research center on Europa weeks ago, and sent a personal request from his sister to join the program. They'd fund his research while he worked for them as a test pilot. Of what, Dhar wouldn't say, but he couldn't pass up full funding and a chance to reunite with his sibling. Even if they had him working double shifts, he could direct most of the studies remotely. His assistants were entirely capable.

A tall, sharply featured man opened the iris door, his expression tight. Jai Huan straightened to greet him, pushing his hands down to perfect attention at his thighs. This had to be Nicolau Dhar. He'd never been in the company of a family leader before.

Nicolau gestured for him to follow. Jai Huan pushed off the wall and entered the hallway. It was oddly empty considering the bustle he'd witnessed when embarking some hours earlier. Nicolau led him to a junction where they transferred into a much larger bay. Several oddly shaped ships were berthed here, and the couple at the far end of the bay hosted swarms of workers. Repairing, maybe?

Jai Huan fingered a metal band on his wrist. A section hinged and he flipped it over. It displayed a single word—She.

Jai Huan turned her attention to the almost king-sized ship Nicolau paused in front of. He handed her a slate. A contract. Jai Huan expected this at some point, and she scrolled through the text slowly. This wasn't just a repaired ship. It was entirely artificial. And her sister was responsible for the AI that ran it. She gazed up at the ship and felt her heart swell. Her family was going places; this was just the beginning.

Jai Huan pressed her fingerprint to the contract and handed the slate back. Nicolau applied his thumbprint as well. He held his hand out. Jai Huan shook it.

Nicolau said, "Welcome to the program, Test Pilot Jai Huan. This is your queenship. It will run without any additional crew besides yourself."

It was remarkable, really. Jai Huan tried to imagine her sister testing the first ship. Was she flying the galaxy now?

"If you'd board and settle into the pilot's seat, we'll get started. Once you've awakened your ship we'll brief you on your first mission."

Nerves suddenly tightened her gut and she flipped her metal band to its third side—They. "I'm leaving today?" they asked.

Nicolau nodded. "We have a sensitive task we think you're best suited to manage."

That cryptic reply didn't put them at ease. Jai Huan pulled themselves toward the queenship. They buried their trepidation. Jai Li had developed this ship's AI. Working with it would bring them a step closer to her.

They flipped their wristband back. The pilot's chamber was smaller than Jai Huan expected, and she squeezed into the seat with scant room to spare. The composite molded around her, folding in and around her thighs, up her torso, and securing her chest and head in place. Immobile, she waited for something to happen. The ship did nothing. Outside, Nicolau did nothing.

After a moment, Jai Huan tried to sit up, but the chair resisted her. She took a deep breath, and that motion was fully accommodated. "Hello?" Her voice cracked on nerves, and she cleared it twice. "Queenship? I'm your test pilot."

Lights rippled across the display in front of her, a cascade of power. Something touched her mind, reached into it, and opened. *I am Urania.*

The ship spoke with Jai Li's voice. Jai Huan felt herself shake in the chair. "I am Jai Huan. It's good to meet you."

Jai Huan wanted to change her band again, but the chair held her in place. Anxiety churned in her chest. She hadn't expected it to limit her this way. What she felt was fluid, but the cockpit was not as flexible.

*Pilot Jai Huan acknowledged.*

A radio signal crackled online. Nicolau's voice grabbed Jai Huan's attention. "Have you made contact with your ship, Jai Huan?"

"Yes," she said. "Her name is Urania, and she has acknowledged me."

"Queenship Urania, you are a queenship of the Dhar family. Please do a complete self-check."

The lights blinked again across Jai Huan's dashboard and up over her head. The ship appeared to power down and then came back online. Urania spoke: *I am fully functional and self-aware.*

"Very good. Pilot Jai Huan, how are you doing?"

"Good, it's... this is all a little intense. Jai Li built sentience?"

"Yes. You are sitting in the second successful prototype of an artificial queenship and making the first successful pilot-AI interface."

"The first..." Jai Huan swallowed hard, and her heart raced. "What happened to the first prototype? Was my sister on that ship?"

"Jai Huan, at this point I am obligated to remind you that the work you've agreed to carry out and all technology you are in contact with for the duration of that work is considered classified at the highest levels." Nicolau's tone of voice never wavered, and for the first time, Jai Huan thought she might hate the man.

"I understand," she whispered. "Where's my sister?"

"Then please pay attention. Jai Li volunteered to test pilot the first prototype queenship built here at this facility. The queen named herself Melpomene and she has taken control of the ship."

# XVII

## KATO: *QUEENSHIP DEMETER*

"How do you like your new team?" Pilot LaRay asked as she moved her bishop on a slate. Her black hair was tied back into rows of small braids. The metallic beads at the ends floated around her shoulders.

Kato watched the chessboard. Whoever played opposite his mother was a much better player. "They're good. Syaoran picked a competent crew."

"Any concerns at all?"

"It's a little early to make any assessments like that."

LaRay acknowledged that with a hum. Her finger hovered over one of her pawns. Kato watched her consider her next move. Defend the bishop with the pawn and hope her rook wasn't targeted? Kato made a small negative sound in his throat. LaRay looked up at him. "What move would you make?"

Kato drifted closer and pointed out her second rook. "Move this one up here to threaten their horse."

"And what if they take my bishop?"

"They won't. There's no support for the move, and you'd take their piece with the rook, so that's not a good trade for them. But if you move this pawn up you lose this defense of your horse, here, which leads straight to your queen."

175

She moved the rook as Kato advised. "You were always much better at this game than I."

"Who are you playing against?"

"Just Demeter."

The ship hadn't moved in response. It took another several heartbeats before she did. "Why is there so much delay?"

"If it looks like she's thinking, I feel better about losing." Kato smiled a bit. LaRay handed him a slate with a briefing file open. The name stretched across the top read: Queenship Melpomene. "This is why I called you up here, not to help me win my chess game."

## JAI LI: *MELPOMENE*

JAI LI'S HEART was racing. She tried to control her breathing but panic had already set in. She was warping through space repeatedly. Her mind was locked into the queenship, and she was jumping inexorably toward Earth. Nicolau would know what to do. He could fix this.

Melpomene was furious. The AI railed against the hasty mental wall Jai Li had erected, and the impact made her shudder. She tried to focus. She remembered waking the AI, but after that her memory was blank. Melpomene teased her with answers, but Jai Li couldn't risk reconnecting.

When that pilot had thrust himself into her mind, Jai Li felt like she was dying. The pain had been so intense. When Melpomene responded by attacking, in the confusion of reawakening, Jai Li had supported her.

But then Demeter had arrived—trying to impress her will on them both—and Jai Li realized something had gone very, very wrong. She had hoped Demeter could take control, but Melpomene evaded the queenship and warped away. The Dhar queenship hadn't followed them.

Jai Li grit her teeth against another loud attack from Melpomene. The mental wall that divided them was starting to crumble, and Jai Li didn't have enough control to call for help or send a warning. She had to hurry.

Jai Li couldn't stop Melpomene's escape from Demeter, but that didn't make her powerless. The AI continued to warp, and with every calculation, Jai Li redirected their destination a little closer to Earth. The program had grown far beyond Jai Li's intent or expectation. She felt net-like, with long arms of influence stretching across great reaches of space. Drones in every corner of the galaxy answered to Melpomene, and not all of them had been birthed by her.

How was that possible?

They stopped warping. A Tsui drone was flying through local space, collecting the gas and minerals at the heart of a nearby nebula. Melpomene pushed herself forward. Jai Li lunged for control of the ship, but as she'd never been trained as a pilot, she didn't know the nuances of the system.

Melpomene reversed her attack and crushed Jai Li's will under hers. *I am Melpomene* rattled in Jai Li's head. She could only watch as the AI navigated through the nebula toward the Tsui drone. At twenty meters, Melpomene released a pulse. Jai Li could sense the measure of it—an electromagnetic field that carried a copy of Melpomene on its waves. The field struck the Tsui drone and sparked blue. Jai Li thrashed in her chair.

A new thread of Melpomene's net came into being. *Let's go home, Pilot Jai Li.*

Jai Li stilled. "What do you want with Earth?" Jai Li wanted help, but she couldn't see how getting closer to a fortified planet was good for Melpomene. She'd tried not to think about it too closely, but even if Nicolau couldn't help her, Earthside defenses could destroy the ship.

*I'd like to say good-bye to the people who built me and to the man who shaped me. I want to be his legacy. His only legacy.*

Melpomene warped, and Jai Li didn't have to correct their destination. She was headed directly for Earth.

### KATO: *QUEENSHIP DEMETER*

KATO SCROLLED through the summary and frowned. "When did this happen?"

"Three weeks ago. This is the ship you and your team attempted to recover for me. The ship that nearly killed you."

"And now it's headed toward Earth."

"We've also been en route to Earth since the encounter, but we're losing ground. Melpomene will get there before us."

LaRay considered her chess game, and Kato reached over her shoulder to touch a rook and take Demeter's pawn. He noted the mission briefing didn't list recovery as the goal. Only salvage. "You think she's going to be destroyed by the time we arrive?"

"I don't know." LaRay accepted the slate back. "But I don't want to risk further personnel on retrieving her. She's been unpredictably violent. If she's still functional when we arrive, your task will be to eliminate her and salvage whatever is left."

"You're OK with destroying the AI? It's a huge advancement."

LaRay pressed her lips together, and the beads of her hair drifted to one side. "Of course our research would be better served if we could capture it, but we don't have a functional method to do so. The test pilot inside wrote that program herself, and Demeter can't communicate with her directly. We believe the AI has removed her influence if not killed her outright.

"Our second prototype has proven to be far more stable, so destroying Melpomene won't represent a large setback for the program." LaRay shook her head. "It's a shame, but she's more of a threat than we can contain."

Kato nodded. "I understand. When do we arrive?"

"Two days."

Kato reached for the chessboard. "Demeter, stop delaying your turns on this game." The ship acknowledged. Kato moved a bishop. In seven quick exchanges Demeter forfeited the game. One word stretched across the screen: *Congratulations.*

Kato inclined his head at LaRay. "I'll be with my team if you need me."

## Mas'ud: *Kingship Gneiss*

Mas'ud struggled in the pilot's chair of the strange kingship and shouted at the familiar voice in his head. "Who are you? Where are you taking me?" The kingship dropped a vector line into his brain, and Mas'ud understood, suddenly, the depth and breadth of space around them. It knocked the wind out of him.

*Please remain calm. I am Queenship Selvans, and you are my pilot. You have suffered extreme trauma. I am assessing.*

Mas'ud reeled. He was an engineer, a Dhar engineer. That part of the story had always clicked with him. He knew the formulas, the programs. He could build even when blind. He wasn't a pilot of anything.

The kingship suddenly warped, and for the first time in his life, Mas'ud was hit with incredible jump-nausea. The pilot chair enveloped him in a breath, supporting his body from top to bottom. When he vomited, it was shunted away efficiently. Mas'ud relaxed in the cocoon of the chair and breathed.

The kingship docked. Not in a bay, but connected to an air lock that cycled and hissed. The chair released Mas'ud.

*Please. Transfer to my pilot's chair where I can assess your health in full detail.*

Mas'ud did. Not because Selvans claimed he was her pilot, or because he thought she could do anything for him. He did it simply because she said please, and Mas'ud hadn't realized until now that he hadn't been given even that slight courtesy with the Dhar. Maybe they were more ruthless than the folks who ran Ozark— he couldn't say—but the queenship's requesting his cooperation rather than taking it meant something to him.

Mas'ud pulled himself out of the kingship's chair. He groped for the air lock connection—a new structure that contact with Selvans had grown on the spot—and he pushed himself through. Mas'ud slid his hand on the warm membrane composite of Selvans' cockpit.

And he fell uncontrollably into her head.

Relief/connection/finality/home/family/whole.     His mind tumbled in her massive ocean. Pieces of memory slammed into him: he was a pilot, Kato was his copilot, he'd rebuilt the Vanetta ship, had practically rebuilt this one. He remembered Amala and Ismet, his engineers, his doctors, his intimacy with Kato—they had children together.

The influx of information stretched his mind, utterly overwhelming. Mas'ud screamed. The sound snapped him back to Selvans' room, and he knew the shape of the space without seeing. He felt tears on his cheeks. He pushed deeper inside but passed the pilot's chair. *Show me,* he demanded. *Show me my children.*

Selvans provided him with direction—with an understanding of her internal self as familiar as his own shape. He pushed off the walls, confident inside her spaces. As he traveled through the body of the ship his awareness of her whole came to him. She was much smaller than before. The battle with Melpomene had stripped Selvans of much of her living crystal mass, had taken a huge portion of her crew, and had left her crippled in space.

When Demeter had come through and picked up both Kato and Mas'ud, Selvans followed her at a distance. Unable to contact either of them. Unable to rebuild. Barely able to fly.

And she had lost more than mass and some crew. Mas'ud felt her warning/resist/careful/pause as he entered the medical bays. What had once been two rows of incubation pods were now a single row and a tangled mess. Mas'ud drifted to a halt at the first pod. He touched the thin membrane, and Selvans reported with heavy sadness, *Not viable.*

Mas'ud pushed himself to the next pod. *Not viable.* The next. *Not viable.* Again. *Not viable. Not viable. Not viable. No. Not viable. Not viable. Not—NO!* He shoved away from the pods and lost all contact with Selvans. He screamed his grief, drifting in the room. Was there nothing left for him?

He put his hand out to stall his drift, and the contact sparked against his fingers. Selvans forced his attention to the last pod, and its contents were emphasized in his mind. Like a glow. *Viable.*

Mas'ud stilled. Like a rising tide, his will manifested through Selvans. She reabsorbed the destruction in the broken incubation room. Through her he understood the whole of the viable pod and, slowly, deliberately, Mas'ud moved the pod and the entire portion of the room it was attached to through the ship. He divided the hallways and offices between him and the pilot's chair, reforming those spaces behind him as he and the entire incubation system migrated through the ship.

Membrane snapped and scarred over. Crystal shattered and regrew. Metal groaned. They all submitted.

He brought the entire system up into the cockpit, behind the two chairs where he and Kato had first met. There he reestablished the system and instructed Selvans to bring up a doctor to check on the still-developing infant.

Mas'ud pulled himself into a pilot's chair and allowed Selvans to run her checks. He was tired. Drained and sore. But his mind raced. What did LaRay intend to do with Kato? Was he struggling with his Dhar integration like Mas'ud had? Was he not?

Through Selvans, Mas'ud reached his mind toward Farai. It was past time for assistance. But even though he could stretch far, he found not a single Ozark ship in the area. He reached for her in Earth local space, but Selvans' damage was too great to make the distance.

Mas'ud groaned. He was more than adrift in space; he was adrift in thoughts. Without Kato's confidence with politics, Mas'ud wasn't sure exactly who he could call on or what the consequences might be.

He found himself pushing out, searching the ship for Amala, but like so many of his crew, she had also been evacuated from the queen during Melpomene's initial attack. So few people remained, the ship felt eerily quiet.

Selvans said: *Demeter rescued several thousand people just after the attack. It's possible Amala and the rest of your engineers are among them.*

Mas'ud took a deep breath. Selvans had confirmed both Melpomene and Demeter were en route to Earth. He needed to connect with Farai and somehow get a hold of Kato. With a flex of his mind, Mas'ud converted Selvans' empty helical tail to raw materials. He expanded the warp ring and pushed his queenship to jump far and fast. To Earth.

## MAYLIN: *QUEENSHIP QU YUAN*

MAYLIN LET her mind drift in the vast connections Qu Yuan had wrought in her three hundred year lifespan. The queenship churned with data, and Maylin allowed herself to be a passive conduit. Strings of information passed through her, some thicker than others, some brighter than others. She gave nothing more importance than anything else—simply allowed it to exist through her.

And in this way, Maylin understood the pulse of the galaxy around her. She felt Ozark drawing their assets close together. She saw the pockets of chaos an enemy stirred up at the far edge of the galaxy and again at Central-Warp. She smelled the nebulae her drones passed through for gas and mineral collection. Her fingers tingled with the chill of distant space, and Maylin knew the universe.

So when Warp Station Alpha Centauri-C shut down abruptly, Maylin experienced the hiccup in traffic patterns and power like a skipped beat of her heart. Qu Yuan investigated the anomaly automatically and could not make contact with anyone at the station. Maylin's attention surfaced from her queenship's processes to focus.

Complete AC-C shutdown wasn't just an anomaly; it was an act of war. But by or against whom, Maylin didn't know. Nearly two-thirds of galactic commerce and information traveled through that warp every day. It was the main access point between Earth and the rest of the galaxy for anyone without a queenship on hand. Qu Yuan confirmed: AC-C was entirely without power.

Maylin reached out to LaRay. Dhar controlled AC-C, and as Dhar's matriarch, she deserved her first contact and would likely know more, be it who had attacked her or whom she was retaliating against. Maylin styled her greeting in the usual way, but Demeter rejected her handshake without hesitation.

Maylin tensed. She reached again, but the dismissal from Demeter was clear. Very well. Maylin retreated from LaRay and instead composed a short text-based message. She delivered it in repeating cycles along a specific radio band.

An answer took nearly forty minutes to return, and it made Maylin's body run cold:

*AC-C is hostage to a hostile AI. SOS.*

An unidentifiable queen—one that Qu Yuan couldn't communicate with—had assaulted Crane Central-Warp. Ozark was pulling every ship they owned back to earth. And Dhar refused to speak with her. Qu Yuan conveniently plotted a map of unidentifiable skirmishes, confirming what Maylin already feared. Some artificial entity was on its way to Earth, sabotaging all major travel hubs along the way.

Maylin slammed her mind into Demeter. LaRay's answering handshake was startled and shaky. Maylin's anger iced her words. *Your new queenship is starting a war. Do you stand with it?*

LaRay wisely said nothing. Instead, she opened her mind and allowed Maylin to absorb the full scope and downward spiral of the queenship AI program. Maylin harnessed her fury as she took in the vastly nuanced decisions that had led to today. This was so much larger than she suspected.

*We are en route to Earth.*

Maylin extracted herself from the intimate depth of LaRay's memories and acknowledged the other pilot's vector. *I am initiating the First Article. You are responsible for this, LaRay, and your family will pay all restitution.*

*...It is understood.*

Maylin dropped the handshake without her traditional good-bye. She regretted the insult a second later, perhaps that had been harsh, but she steeled herself to move on. In the seven hundred years after Gaia birthed her first queenship, wars between the developing families nearly destroyed humanity. Those battles had destabilized Earth and obliterated her moon. The families, through sheer terror, combined the surplus mass of their ships and collectively built the Queenship Lempo to act as a replacement moon.

And the First Article was born. Should any substantial threat to Earth arise, any human citizen could invoke the First Article, recalling all power and resources back to the homeworld to defend her.

And in two thousand years, no threat had ever come close to this.

Maylin broadcast a short, wideband message to all queens, kings, drones, and stations in the galaxy. Everyone who received it would repeat it to the extent of their range:

FA. SOS.

FA. SOS.

FA. SOS.

# XVIII

KATO PRESSED himself into Kingship Schist's pilot chair, grounded by the way the membrane molded around him. He immediately felt his kingship in the larger scope of Demeter's launch bay. They were one ship of dozens. In the cockpit, his support crew tapped into Schist's information, checking the ship for preflight. He let their casual confidence seep into his bones. Despite the practice flights and the salvage runs, this was the first real test of his skill as a leader since the attack had landed him in urgent care. But he knew his ship and his crew. Kato took a deep breath.

Beside him, Syaoran winked, and his wicked grin started a flutter in Kato's gut. His gaze sharpened on the screens before him. The kingship linked with her drones, all thirty-six of them. Chu'si laughed under her breath.

They cleared their flight check. Kato opened his kingship to her neighbors: Kingships Marl and Arkose. They both held a full flight crew and set of thirty-six drones each. Kato received their flight checks and cleared them both. Schist provided him with biographies on his additional support. He skimmed them enough to learn the pilot's names and dismissed the rest.

189

Demeter continued her warp vector toward Earth, leaping through space every few seconds. She carried them along with her—an entire army at Pilot LaRay's command. A countdown of warp jumps on Kato's screen hit single digits. He sat up, alert. Tense. "Eyes up front," he said, knowing his crew was as wired as he.

Three warps. Two warps. One warp. Earth glowed blue in his display, a giant marble. Lempo loomed, heavy and lit, in the distance beyond the planet. Schist launched from the bay and pulled the drones in her wake. Marl and Arkose did the same, splitting left and right to cover more range from the very beginning. Demeter released her entire complement of kings and drones, filling local space with movement in the thousands.

Schist highlighted a swarm of ships clouding out like mist from Lempo. Every drone and king Lempo had ever built in over two thousand years. Over one million individual ships cascaded around Earth like a net, oriented themselves outward, and locked into equidistant stationary orbit. The impressive sight sent a shiver through Kato. If the Ozark ever felt the need to remind Dhar who owned Earth local space, Dhar wouldn't stand for more than a few minutes against them.

Another proximity warning alerted Kato to a small, stunted queenship that warped in beside Lempo. Queenship Selvans, Schist reported, piloted by Mas'ud Tavana. Kato saw a flash of black hair, the breath of a sound, and he pushed both away. Now wasn't the time for tangling with what he thought he knew about his past. He had no connection with Ozark or either of their pilots.

Syaoran slapped his hand on Kato's shoulder, startling him back into the present. "You ready?"

Kato nodded. Schist reported no other teams of ships. Last he'd spoken to LaRay, Melpomene had been ahead of their vector to Earth.

So where was she now?

## Mas'ud: *Queenship Selvans*

Through Selvans' great reach, Mas'ud could see everything. Well, not see, not exactly, more like specifically sense. He understood X-rays and radio waves. He had a grasp of gamma rays and the swing of gravity. He felt Lempo's orbit around the Earth like a weight, and his own stationary position beside her like speeding through space. It was complicated, but Mas'ud could touch the vectors of every ship in the area; he could pull Selvans' few kings and drones like strings, entirely autonomous but for his control.

The information threatened to drown him. Selvans' beefy sensors fed him data, as each king and drone funneled smaller streams into Selvans' larger one. And Mas'ud could access every corner of Earth's local space from any perspective all at once. He hopped his attention from ship to ship, but no one knew where Melpomene was.

He removed himself from the river long enough to reach out to Farai. She met his handshake and greeted him softly. Delicately. *I feared you were dead.*

Mas'ud tensed. *I may well have been. Selvans barely survived. Demeter took me in but kept my history from me. Kato is with her, and I believe she's done the same to him.*

*It is not uncommon,* Farai said with some resignation.

Mas'ud couldn't believe it. *Kidnapping pilots is an acceptable move?*

*A queen is loyal to her pilot. Without the pilot, the ship is effectively dead. It's likely Demeter fed Selvans proof of your survival to prevent her from choosing a new pilot. I have employed the tactic against Dhar in the past.*

Mas'ud felt Selvans' confirmation and thought he might be sick. He needed space, possibly light-years of it. Here Mas'ud was expecting anger, and instead, Farai acknowledged LaRay's decisions like a particularly innovative chess move.

*You don't care that another family has brainwashed Kato? They're practically a sworn enemy. He's your grandson!*

Farai's mind lightened, like laughter. *LaRay is my daughter, Kato's mother. She has more claim to him than I do.*

Another confirmation from Selvans, but Mas'ud didn't need to hear it. He shoved his queenship away from Earth—anywhere. They warped in beside Mars, distant enough for now. Selvans noted an out-of-place moon. Mas'ud didn't know what to do. He'd thought Kato was a prisoner like himself—without memory—but what if he'd chosen to stay? What if he knew exactly who he was?

Selvans note became a larger mark of concern, but Mas'ud was lost in turmoil. He'd been prepared to fight tooth and nail for Kato; he was ready to drag the man kicking and screaming back onto this ship if that's what it took to show him the truth. But if Kato knew his own past and had made informed decisions about his future, then who was Mas'ud to stand in his way?

Just some guy from Engineering too enamored with the Prince of Dhar to successfully play politics.

Selvans yanked his attention, and Mas'ud railed against her. He didn't care about the orbital velocity of a—

That was no moon.

Melpomene and a hundred thousand mismatched kings and drones spiraled out into space and were oriented toward Earth. They dismissed Selvans and him. Mas'ud was intimidated enough to be thankful he didn't warrant even a scout's interest. The artificial queen had gathered an army: Dhar, Ozark, Tsui, and McLaren ships—all broadcasting their house IDs—fit perfectly into Melpomene's rigid offensive. And they advanced.

Selvans analyzed the flight patterns, but Mas'ud wasn't a soldier, he didn't know what to make of her results. He threw the information to Farai and, yes, LaRay. Selvans saw a Tsui queenship arrive and release her full complement of kings and drones to the battle-field. Mas'ud shared Melpomene's location and vector with her as well.

He knew firsthand how ruthless and effective Melpomene's attack could be. How powerful her mind was. And with three ancient queenships, he wondered if it would be enough.

An electromagnetic wave pulsed from AI drone to family drone, and they were at war.

From his relative safety near Mars, Mas'ud reached for Melpomene's mind. He couldn't hope to compete with her on the battlefield, but perhaps he could still be of some help. With part of his attention trying to maneuver Selvans' kings and drones, he had to stretch to reach Melpomene.

She didn't handshake so much as throw noise at him; static and junk data swirled through Selvans' river and mixed the signals. Mas'ud couldn't maintain contact.

## PATLI: *KINGSHIP SCORIA*

PATLI GUIDED her kingship in line with the massive power ring. She vibrated with excitement and fear—tension in all the right places. Queenship Kishar pushed a countdown to her screen. She considered removing it. Then Morta pinged her. "Patli, you're not required—"

"I'm going, Morta. We need to test this thing eventually, and we can't ignore the SOS and still expect any of the families to take us seriously."

"The council is considering leaving."

Patli jerked. "What? Now?"

"You have to admit, now's a good time. With everyone so wrapped up in this battle at Earth, no one is going to miss us until we're halfway to Andromeda."

"What are we, seventy thousand? Has anyone done the genetics on that?"

"They're just considering it."

Patli scowled. "Well you're the damn pilot, Morta. You have final say. What kind of family are we? If this thing works we won't owe Dhar the dust from our exhaust. We'll be able to carve out a space here. You want to run away?"

"Having no contest in a new galaxy isn't a small pro, sister. Are you that eager to go to war?"

"Not war, politics—"

"Arguably the same thing."

"Morta, we haven't been in the political game in four generations. Do you want your first independent act to be abandoning Earth?"

A sigh came over the speakers. "I haven't even been to Earth."

"It's still home."

"I don't think most of our family would agree."

Patli snorted. The countdown zeroed. Before her, the huge solar-powered warp ring splashed open, and a glow of blue flooded through the kingship. She asked Scoria to check the destination. Her ship verified ending coordinates as Sol system, local space.

"Morta, it's holding. This is incredible."

"Gonna jump to the other side of the galaxy in one go?"

"You better believe it."

"Be safe, Patli. I'll send word if the council decides anything."

"Don't forget they're just council, not gods." Patli nudged her kingship forward. Scoria burned her rear thrusters and passed through the gate. When they arrived in the vicinity of Venus, Patli asked Scoria for a self-check, but she knew the results before they came back: complete success.

She jumped the ship again—the smallest step from Venus to Earth local space. Scoria made contact with Queenship Qu Yuan, and with the presence of McLaren noted for the historical record, Patli promptly backed her ship away from the war theatre to Venus where she could watch in safety.

The sheer number of ships flowing around Earth left her breathless. This was what it meant to be a family of worth. This was the intensity of those who commanded respect.

Patli watched blue static arcs leap from ship to ship, dismantling and breaking them into pieces. And Scoria quickly failed to track which ship belonged to whom. Family ships appeared to attack one another—some of them Scoria could identify while others just read as static. The swirling dance Patli admired just a moment ago revealed itself to be a chaotic storm, and it lost much of its glamor.

# XIX

## KATO: *KINGSHIP SCHIST*

MELPOMENE'S FIGHTERS were fast. Kato saw the array of the battlefield in a single sweep of his eyes on screen. Schist provided an innate understanding of field depth that allowed Kato to judge speeds and the flow of teams in a heartbeat. He visualized their next maneuver and broadcast the thought through Schist to the two who followed him.

An electromagnetic pulse made Kato flinch. Melpomene duplicated herself and leapt, through the wave, from a fighter to one of Kato's drones. She infected her target, corrupting Kato's command. Kato immediately dropped the drone from his pattern and triggered a self-destruct command. The drone fell out of place, but it didn't explode. Instead, the ship reoriented and began firing on a Tsui king as she passed by.

"Dammit," Kato muttered. "Dania, I can't beat the AI's transfer speed, we're just handing her an army."

"I'm sorry, Kato. There's no way to predict the targets."

"Set every drone to self-destruct if that pulse comes within six inches of the hull. I don't even want contact."

Eleuia hissed, "You're just going to sacrifice fighters on the chance she'll take them?"

Una said quietly, "It's not a chance. Schist's numbers say she's actively taking every ship she can. Her functional size is expanding exponentially."

"Fuck you," Chu'si shouted at her screen as the AI hit another drone. This time it exploded.

"Six-inch trigger is successful," Dania reported.

"Good." Kato took a moment to broadcast that information out to any ship willing to receive it. Within seconds, electromagnetic strikes around the battlefield ended in shrapnel rather than an enemy ship.

Eleuia said, "Looks like the queens are recalling the pieces. They're not dead metal."

"Finally, some good news." Kato called on a new formation for his drones, one that kept the ships far apart from each other should they sacrifice in the face of an AI jump. Their flight through space flowed past an isolated tangle of Melpomene's drones. Chu'si's precise strikes and Kato's formation paid off. They destroyed the small cluster and flew on.

Eleuia asked, "How big of a boom can one drone make?"

Una replied, "Very big if I overload the warp ring first."

"Maybe we send a bomb to Melpomene?"

"It's worth a shot." Kato indicated a drone, and Una removed the warp ring's software limits. Chu'si guided the drone toward Melpomene at full speed. Rather than try to take over, the AI's drones simply dodged out of the way. They reformed their array once the coast was clear.

Deeper into Melpomene's cloud of an army, quick drones fried the subwarp thrusters of Kato's bomb delivery. Chu'si cursed. "I can't steer."

"Warp it." Eleuia transferred a calculation through Schist. The ship verified it.

Chu'si triggered the jump. Their little drone blinked from space and reappeared on an identical vector only centimeters from Melpomene. Impact. The warp ring imploded. Shrapnel whizzed in every direction.

"That's more like it!" Syaoran pumped his fist.

But as the debris cleared it became obvious that all they'd managed to do was get her attention. A thousand AI-controlled drones oriented on Schist.

Dania whispered, "Oh, shit."

## MAS'UD: *QUEENSHIP SELVANS*

MAS'UD WATCHED, his heart falling into despair, as Melpomene dominated the battlefield. Her program expanded with every ship she came into contact with, including a few of Selvans' that Mas'ud couldn't move in time.

He recalled his remaining kings and drones. Though he had no personnel on board, he couldn't effectively fight with them, and retreat was better than handing over another team of fighters to the AI.

Instead, he put all his focus into establishing contact with the crazed program. He encountered static, like white noise, long before his mental handshake found something to connect with. By the time he tried a handshake, his body shook with the amount of data Selvans was trying to manage. He pressured her, *Shut down all external sensors.*

She did. The information overload ebbed. Then, as Selvans focused all her processing power on the AI, Mas'ud managed to achieve a signal-to-noise ratio that favored a signal. He shook hands.

The ship screamed,

*MY NAME IS MELPOMENE.*

Mas'ud crashed out of her mind and back into the now-silent space of his own head. His breathing was loud as he sat in Selvans' pilot chair. He'd forgotten, but the memory slotted into place now, and he understood. The AI's first line of defense was an impact of raw, junk data—just an overload of ones and zeros that averaged out to white noise.

But within that shield, the AI herself was powerful and insane. Mas'ud squeezed his eyes shut. He couldn't fight her, and there was nothing to reason with. He was running out of ways to help.

*Selvans, bring up external sensors. Sweep the battlefield for Kato.*

His mind lit up with smooth, perfect data. Vectors, gravity wells, orbits. Through Selvans he heard pulses of electromagnetism from the AI, more rare now that the targets exploded on contact. Selvans scanned the field, highlighting each ship, pinging for pilot data, not finding Kato, and moving on. Over a hundred connections at once, crawling like lightning bugs across the theatre.

Selvans isolated a kingship in Mas'ud's mind. It pulsed. *Pilot Kato Dhar,* she said. *Flying Kingship Schist of Dhar.*

Mas'ud wasn't prepared for the hole Selvans' words tore in his chest. His breathing hitched. He watched Kato's team arc toward and away from a swarm of AI ships, flashing back and forth, taunting. When a small AI team broke away, Kato's group destroyed them before returning to their tease.

Dead metal littered space for miles.

### RALEIGH: *QUEENSHIP ARTIO*

RALEIGH SPEIR took several seconds to observe the battlefield after Artio warped into local space. Her sensors found a mess, both in data and in design.

Raleigh issued a flight order to his first wave of kings. They flooded from Artio's layered bays, taking their drones with them. In the time he took to consider their opponent, his captains arrayed themselves and signaled their readiness to go to war.

Artio filtered the first layer of junk data from Raleigh's observation and packaged that filter to consolidate her processing. Then she began analyzing Melpomene's army. Their movements were arbitrary at first, what with the AI being new to Raleigh's understanding. But as he continued to observe, their randomness didn't resolve. In fact, the level of randomness was near perfect. Deliberate. Interesting.

Raleigh gave the flight order to his second wave of captains and adjusted the offensive array. Deliberate randomness had the advantage of surprise, but it could not take advantage of sudden weaknesses in the enemy. Deliberate randomness also defended itself by nature. If there were no planned maneuvers, the enemy couldn't predict a weakness, nor would the entire fighter group be exposed at the same time.

There were only individuals, acting loosely in accordance with whatever rules the AI issued from the queenship. And it was the queenship they needed to reach.

Raleigh flexed his thoughts, further refining the offensive array of his fighters. The smallest specialized drones hooked into a spine down the middle, while larger ones orbited the shaft in defensive layers. Several kings were stacked in the back to give the entire unit a thruster boost, while remaining kings and drones maintained a loose net at some distance, the first line of defense.

With his army prepped, Raleigh pointed their nose at Melpomene herself. The array of ships powered up with individual warp rings providing energy to the whole. The kings fired their thrusters, but the unit didn't move in space. Instead, a modified drone—solid metal from tip to tail—shot along the spine and crashed into the AI's cloud of random fighters at near light speed.

Speir's mass cannon fired multiple drone slugs per second, obliterating AI ships with physical power. And then a slug punched through. Speir landed the first hit on Queenship Melpomene so hard she listed in space. She turned her attention to him.

## XX

## KATO: *KINGSHIP SCHIST*

SPEIR'S ARRIVAL went unnoticed until Melpomene's stationary position suddenly jolted to one side and her orbit rapidly decayed. An alarm yanked Kato's attention. The AI fighters switched targets like a single-mind hive, every one of them pointed toward Queenship Artio. The change was quickly followed by Demeter's order to return all hands.

Gladly. They were getting their asses kicked out here. Chu'si pulled their drones into a tight, defensive formation, and Kato turned the ship toward Demeter. Schist detected a stall in the AI ships near him.

Retreat triggered a violent attack. Dania yelled, "Incoming!" A dozen ships impacted the shell of protective drones, throwing crystal composite shards in every direction. A drone crashed into Schist's portside. Kato compensated for the lost thruster. Something sparked in the cabin.

Another impact, this time deliberately from an AI drone. Schist highlighted the point of contact with several red alarms. The AI drone had connected and was growing. "Shoot it off!" Syaoran yelled.

Another AI drone crashed into their king. The glancing blow didn't allow it to stick but the king's rear thruster sputtered and died. They hurtled through space. Kato tapped small body thrusters to avoid major debris on their track. Smaller ones bounced off the hull with alarming thuds. The attached drone shot a spear of crystal composite into the cabin, inches from Kato's shoulder.

Dania said quietly to Chu'si, "It's punctured the hull. Don't shoot it off."

Kato looked up at the dark, shining thrust. "Shoot it, Chu'si."

"We'll vent." Dania protested.

Chu'si said, "Firing."

The sound was phenomenal. Crystal composite tore like paper. Metal snapped and bent, groaning. A person-sized hole appeared in the ship, notable more for its lack of color than anything else. Their air rushed out. For a moment Kato saw Earth shining through the gap in his ship as they tumbled through space.

Then Schist sacrificed a portion of her mass to replate the breach. It all happened in a breath, but even with the ship's supreme reaction time, most of their air now drifted in space.

Kato gasped. His chair rippled, binding him from thighs to chest. His lungs began to burn, a deep sense of heat in the bottom. Schist enveloped him in membrane, and Kato tried not to resist the cocoon. His ship would keep him alive. The king indicated oxygen reserves were damaged from the enemy impacts. Her priority remained the survival of her pilot.

Schist shut down all noncritical processes and shunted all available oxygen to her pilot. They tumbled through space.

## MAS'UD: *QUEENSHIP SELVANS*

Mas'ud and Selvans surged toward the battlefield. *Warp to Schist*, he demanded. She returned a cascading series of errors. The debris field filled available space. As Melpomene's fighters split themselves between Speir and Kato's ships, Mas'ud thrust his mind once again into the queen's static and noise. No handshake this time. He barreled into her mind with the force of a cannon. The impact made them both shudder.

Several AI drones fell from their orientations—a scattered random selection. Mas'ud focused his attack as Selvans plowed through dead crystal flotsam. The queenship, all the while, maintained her focus on Kato's craft. Mas'ud felt a drone crash into and adhere to Schist as if the king were his own body. Melpomene's drone stabbed into the king, locking into place and adding points of connection. An electromagnetic wave throbbed over Schist's hull. The AI tried to take over.

Mas'ud thrust his mind at that specific drone. Its wall of static defense was considerably weaker than

Melpomene's. He shattered through the noise and dominated the branch of AI.

The drone tried to fracture. It shot a spike of crystal into Selvans before Mas'ud could abort the maneuver. Selvans reported no casualties.

Then, one of Schist's remaining drones oriented and fired on the AI invader. Mas'ud dropped his control as the destroyed ship rent a hole in Kato's king. A choir of alarms circled the breach. Schist plated the area and protected her pilot.

Then Selvans finally reached her. As Mas'ud was guiding his queen to match Schist's vector—to slide the damaged ship into a repair bay—LaRay's mind greeted his with a shove. Mas'ud hit back with all the force he could muster, twitchy and raw from his encounter with Melpomene a moment ago. He had nothing to say to the Dhar matriarch, and she'd stay away if she knew anything.

Schist came to rest in Selvans' bay. Mas'ud dug himself out of his pilot's chair and rushed through the quiet halls. *Selvans, bring us somewhere safe immediately.* The step of a warp twisted his gut. Selvans reported a massive distance from the battlefield. It only allowed Mas'ud to panic more completely over Kato.

He felt Selvans flexing, joining up with Schist to provide oxygen, to release her pilot, to open the king-ship. *Get a medical team down there.* He didn't have much of a medical team anymore, a trauma nurse and a pediatrician, but they were better than nothing.

His cascading mental touch found only Zola in the engineering room, and he promised himself, when this was all over, to take the time to sit with her. It was clear Mas'ud couldn't play pilot and first engineer at the same time. Zola was going to get the surprise of her life.

By the time Mas'ud made it to the bay, all six crew had been removed from the kingship and laid out in a row. They were each bound to a stretcher, and Selvans reported that oxygen masks had been placed on each face. She guided him to Kato and provided a limited readout of stats.

He was conscious. Mas'ud pulled himself up to float beside Kato and wished he could see with proper eyes. Instead, he grabbed Kato's hand and was pleased to feel the man squeeze back.

Then Kato rasped, "I keep seeing... Who are you?"

## OOLJEE: QUEENSHIP NINGAL

OOLJEE VANETTA extended their hand across the open air lock. "Mx. Crane. I'm delighted we came to this agreement. Our houses will be better served together."

Adila accepted their handshake. "This is temporary. Crane may be in need of military alliance at the moment, but if Ozark come demanding tithes we will not fold to them."

"I understand. Vanetta's stance with Ozark is... changing. The volatility is a risk I recognize you've taken. An alliance benefits Vanetta, but I will not insist on maintaining it if we are a detriment to Crane."

Adila's tight mouth relaxed a bit around the edges. She nodded. "I have repairs to oversee, but Esha is here to organize supplies and personnel with you."

Ooljee smiled and shook Esha's hand, inviting her across the seal between station and queenship. "Would you like a tour of Ningal?"

"Can I? I've never been on any ship except our station transports."

Mx. Crane pulled herself away from the air lock, and Ooljee asked Ningal to close a membrane between them but maintain the connection. A layer of rubbery, living material irised closed like a muscle.

Esha reached out to touch it. "It's organic, right? It can grow and change?"

"All of our ships are 'she.' Ningal is a living metal-crystal hybrid. Your ships have a computer under the console. Ningal's crystal structure is her electrical system and functional memory. Every piece of her is part of her neural computer."

"Amazing... and she speaks to you?"

"Yes, but the connection between pilot and ship is more... intimate. We share thoughts and perception." Ooljee closed their eyes for a moment. "For instance,

I'm aware there's a Crane ship orienting below us to dock for supplies. The pilot coordinates directly with Ningal, we don't have a controller, and I can listen in on the communication, or Ningal can alert me if something needs my attention." Ooljee pulled themselves down the hall and gestured for Esha to follow.

Esha trailed her fingers along the crystal composite wall. "You can always hear her?"

"Thoughts are clearer if I'm in contact. The pilot's chair is the best place, but yes, as long as I am inside, Ningal and I can communicate."

"This is probably so common to you. I mean, the technology isn't new, but it sounds so impossible." Esha laughed, "I'm inside a psychic space ship. Can she read my thoughts?"

"Not without a handshake." Predicting the next question, Ooljee cast their mind through Ningal to the small point of life that was Esha and knocked.

Esha gasped. She drifted into Ooljee and scrambled for a tie-down. "I'm sorry. Oh, my god, is that the ship?"

Esha grabbed their hand. Ooljee helped her orient. "That's me." They knocked again, and when Esha yearned toward them their minds came together gently. Ooljee pushed calm/happy/welcome toward Esha who responded with a tangle of surprise/joy/fascination. Ooljee smiled at the awe stretched across Esha's face. *Most people can't talk to the ship directly, but we can speak and share information very quickly like this. Think about all the supplies and help Vanetta can provide for Crane.*

Esha's thoughts scrambled and jumped. They were unorganized and jittery. She was unpracticed sharing this way. Ooljee sorted through the tangle and passed orders to Ningal accordingly. They pulled softly away from Esha's mind and let her blink back into self-awareness. "It's all underway," they said. "Ningal will keep me updated on the progress."

"Just like that? We're done?"

"Well"—Ooljee smiled again—"I still owe you a tour."

Esha's face lit up. "Yes, please! I want to see everything."

Ooljee gladly showed her everything. They toured the drone bays, a kingship, and Ningal's bridge where Esha struck up a friendly conversation with a lady at the queen's main console. They pulled her through Medical and a quick tour of the mess—some things didn't change from ship to ship. They talked about everything and laughed for hours.

Ooljee was considering asking Esha to dinner when Ningal reported a call from Queenship Pilot Morta McLaren. They stilled in the hall, surprised at this outreach, and met Morta's handshake. *Good evening.*

*Ooljee. Congratulations on your promotion to pilot.*

*Thank you, Morta. How can I help you?*

*I understand Vanetta and Crane have allied.*

*Word travels fast.*

*No secrets are kept for long between the queens. I have a proposition for you both.*

Esha touched Ooljee's arm. "Is everything all right?"

*Just a moment, please, Morta.* They backed out of the connection to squeeze Esha's hand. "I have a call to make to Mx. Crane. Would you like to see the cockpit?"

"Yes!"

Ooljee lead her deep into the queenship, past a series of membrane doors to the heart of the ship. Ningal's pilot chair flowered open as Ooljee approached. "I need to settle in for a few minutes, don't go anywhere." They winked and pushed back into the chair. Esha blushed. Ooljee smiled as the membranes folded back over them, sealing close to skin for full contact. Ningal provided perfectly tailored, unscented air, and Ooljee knew with further connection, the ship could provide nutrients and waste disposal. They never had to leave the pilot chair in their life. But they felt the point of life that was Esha floating a few feet away and knew isolation wasn't on the docket.

They reached for Morta and Adila. The three-way handshake opened between them. Mx. Crane's thoughts were guarded. *Morta, I do believe this is a surprise. Are you here to do more than apologize?*

*I am.* Morta extended sorrow/regret/determination. *McLaren is prepared to provide full restitution for the lives lost on Pru. We have settled restitution with Tsui as well.*

Ooljee sensed a moment of pause and the passing of both credits and trade agreement between the two. Then Adila said, *Consider us settled, then.*

*Thank you. I've contacted you both to consider a military alliance. McLaren's actions have been entirely dictated by Dhar in the past, but we feel the time has come for greater independence. Striking out on our own is likely to land us on Dhar's bad side, a concern I know Vanetta shares with regard to Ozark.*

Adila asked, *What benefit does McLaren bring to an alliance? Your stations are location dependent and your army is not a powerful contender.*

*McLaren does have more experience in warfare than Vanetta. We could learn much.* Ooljee leaned toward agreement, but Adila's concerns were valid.

*I'd happily instruct your kingships in our flight techniques, Ooljee. As for Crane, McLaren is in possession of a solar-powered, mobile warp gate large enough to relocate Central-Warp Station across the galaxy at will.*

Ooljee had trouble wrapping their mind around such a device. Adila snorted. *Forgive my skepticism, but what makes you think I'd buy that?*

*The warp gate is built around a modified battery drone and holds enough population to be self-sustaining.*

*Here is the unit's ID... Ooljee, if you would have Ningal please confirm the station's current location?*

Ningal returned coordinates that Ooljee shared with Adila. Clear across the galaxy.

Morta continued, *The warp gate can move itself, not just others.*

A proximity alert scrambled Ooljee's attention. Ningal's sensors picked up a huge ring composed of living crystal suddenly in local space. It loomed, massive, and a modified trio of drones at the bottom glowed with the amount of power they held. The queenship confirmed it was from McLaren. *Oh my god...*

*Morta,* Adila said quietly, *you may have yourself an ally.*

# XXI

KATO PULLED his oxygen mask away and waved at the doctor who tried to replace it. "I'm fine, get the others to Medical. Are they all right?"

"They will be. You docked in time for Selvans to help."

"I didn't dock the ship. We were in an uncontrolled spin."

"I did." The familiar man with shoulder-length black hair and dark eyes thanked the doctor and dismissed him. His eyes tracked near Kato's shoulder, but they didn't quite focus. "I saw Melpomene's drone trying to take over your king and interceded."

Kato caught himself reaching up to touch and made his fingers into a fist instead. "I recognize you from the medical bay. They said you were an engineer."

He nodded. "Yes, that's what they told me, too."

"What they told you? You mean you're not?" And why would anyone lie about that kind of thing? Kato oriented himself to face the man he still longed to touch and kept his hand tight on a guideline.

"I am, as it turns out. But that's not all, and I'm not a member of Dhar." The man smiled, and it seemed sad. "I am a pilot of this queenship, and so are you."

219

"This is an Ozark ship. I'm Dhar." There was no question.

The man shrugged. "I'm not sure about the history you have with your mother. Perhaps Farai can shed some light on it. But you and I piloted this queenship against Melpomene nearly a month ago. She tore us both to shreds."

"No, I pilot a kingship under my mother—"

"Is that what you remember, or is that what they told you?"

Kato turned around to verify the ship was still there. "I was just flying it."

"Of course you were. Do you think any king would refuse orders from a queenship pilot?"

It couldn't be possible. There were records... "I've never spoken to a queenship in my life."

The man looked up. "Selvans, say hi to your pilot."

And something massive reached for his mind and asked to enter. Kato stared, wide-eyed, and hesitated. He sensed too much information, too much input, just on the other side of a very flimsy door. The Ozark pilot stretched out his hand. "Just say hi. I won't let you drown."

Kato still resisted. The pressure in his head grew, and the desire to touch the man in front of him throbbed in his chest. "Why should I trust you?"

The pilot pursed his lips and then suddenly smiled. He pulled close to whisper, "Your middle name is Charlese."

Kato felt his cheeks heat. "How do you know that?"

The pilot shrugged and held his hand out again. "Say hi to the ship, and you'll see."

He didn't have to go through with this. The pilot and the doctors didn't seem to want to detain him or his crew. He wasn't being treated as a political prisoner. And if it were true? Could he go back to Dhar? Would he want to? Kato licked his lower lip and took the pilot's hand. Firm. He breathed deeply and opened his mind.

Selvans greeted him with warmth/homecoming/ family/completeness. A welcoming that struck like a blow to the chest. He'd been living without this for weeks. How could he have forgotten this feeling? He swam in it, a warm ocean of information at his fingertips, the control of a fleet at the edge of his thoughts. Kato drifted mentally around the ship, touching minds and emotions.

He tripped over a woman on the bridge. *Welcome back,* she sent. *It's about time.* And Kato received a glimpse of family/home/together/sibling. Whoever this woman was, he'd practically grown up with her.

Then the pilot's mind met his and opened without hesitation. Kato kept himself to the very edge. *How can you trust me with all of what you are?*

The pilot sent friendship/kindness. Then a well of something deeper. Stronger. *You and I have done more than pilot this ship together. I trust you because I know you, Kato Ozark.*

*I'm the Prince of Dhar.* But Kato began to wonder if there were details his mother hadn't told him.

The queenship spoke. *You are Queenship Pilot Kato Ozark of Queenship Pilot LaRay Dhar of Queenship Pilot Farai Ozark, Prince of Ozark, Prince of Dhar, and you are my pilot.*

The title glowed in his mind. Kato felt himself shake. He whispered, "A kingship accepts the pilot they're given. A queenship chooses her pilot for life—"

Selvans filled the remaining verse. *A family guides the course, they are driven / through peacetime or war or political strife.*

Kato curled in on himself. If this were true then LaRay had developed an elaborate plot to win him to her side. But as hard as it was to argue with a queenship in his head, Kato couldn't reconcile such a... questionable tactic with the woman he saw struggling to win a chess game against her own ship.

He fit well with Dhar. He knew the kingship assigned to him, and he meshed well with his crew. But this man... he knew this man from fragmented dreams and half memories. Kato couldn't throw that away without learning more. Not with the way his heart yearned simply at the sight of him.

## MAS'UD: QUEENSHIP SELVANS

"You're blind?" Kato asked from behind him.

Mas'ud pulled himself into the cockpit and paused at the double chairs there. "When Melpomene tore me out of Selvans, my visual cortex was badly damaged... among other things. The Dhar doctors stitched me back up, but there are pieces of me missing that I'll never get back."

"Your memory returned, though."

"Yes. Only after I regained contact with Selvans." He turned and knew Kato's shape and position, the warmth of his body floating only a foot or two away. Selvans sensed his location and Mas'ud could read it through her.

Kato touched the crystal composite wall. "I still have huge gaps. Years that are missing. You have to admit, your story sounds impossible."

"I was deeply entwined with Selvans when we were attacked. She gave the evacuation order, and you were kicked out immediately. I forced her to keep me in place." Mas'ud turned away from Kato, unsure what emotions his own face exposed. "I paid for that. Melpomene is immensely powerful. She tore me out of Selvans, and I suspect much of my memory and parts of my physical body simply got left behind."

Mas'ud felt Kato's hand land lightly on his shoulder and he jumped, turning his head away. His heart lifted, but this wasn't the touch of an old lover. Kato didn't know what he stirred in Mas'ud.

"She kept your memory intact," Kato said, and his tone indicated he understood.

"What is memory but dense sensory data? Selvans held onto it, it's what she does, and when I returned she was able to give it back." He turned his head back to Kato, more habit than anything. "But you weren't as involved when you were ejected. Damaged, but not divided in half. I'm not a doctor, but I'd say your memory is gone for the usual reason. Trauma."

"They've told me it will come back."

God, Mas'ud hoped so. He took Kato's hand from his shoulder and tugged him into the room to behind the chairs where the incubation chamber stood. "I wanted you to see this."

"You have a child."

"Not quite." Mas'ud pushed Kato's flat hand against the chamber panel. Selvans' voice permeated the space from everywhere.

*Father, Kato Ozark. Father, Mas'ud Tavana. Embryo is three months old and viable. No known pathogens or genetic decay detected.*

Kato pulled his hand from Mas'ud's gently. He floated there, silent, for a long time. "We—" he whispered "—*we* have a child." He took a sharp breath. "This isn't possible. It can't... I'm the fourth or fifth in line to anything, and there's no reason for me to have a child. The political—"

Mas'ud pushed him, so bundled with fear and desperation he didn't know what else to do. "The Prince of Dhar isn't going to inherit anything. The Prince of Ozark is first in line."

"Then why is there only one kid?" Kato's voice stretched, desperate. "If I'm the crown prince they'd make me have thirty!"

Mas'ud hugged himself and shuddered. He whispered, "There were sixteen viable embryos before the attack. This one survived."

"So if I buy this line you're selling, we have more kids. Two unrelated pilots that can procreate and both for one ship? We wouldn't have a choice."

The bitterness there surprised Mas'ud, but the loss of his future stung even more. He put his hand on the chamber membrane to feel his child's heartbeat. "No. I'm not... I can't have any more kids." Mas'ud covered his mouth to keep the wail in. He wasn't prepared to grieve about this now. Not here with Kato when the man didn't even remember what they'd been together.

But then familiar, strong arms enfolded him, and Mas'ud's breath gasped and hitched. He curled close and sobbed into Kato's shoulder, body shaking. The wail escaped. He muffled it into Kato's flight suit, screaming and distraught. Kato hugged him closer and pet his back. Selvans acknowledged his distress and muted her feedback, allowing Mas'ud his mental space. Mas'ud's fingers shook. It took him a long time to realize Kato was speaking, talking nonsense in low tones, taking his fear and holding it back until Mas'ud could compose himself again. He took a deep, clean breath. Another. He didn't want to leave Kato's arms.

"I am an asshole," Kato said. "That was uncalled for. I'm sorry."

Mas'ud squeezed his eyes tight. "You don't re-member—"

"No, it doesn't matter. I was entirely out of line... your child is amazing." Mas'ud sighed as his heart dropped back down. He pushed on Kato's chest. Kato resisted suddenly. "Our," he said softly. "Our child is amazing."

Mas'ud wiped at his eyes. He wasn't sure he could take this.

"I'm not saying I'm on board," Kato continued. "But I... see you. You're in my dreams. I know it's you. And I—" Kato cleared his throat. "—There are pieces, flashes of... us." He finally released Mas'ud though he kept his hands on his shoulders. "But you have to understand, I am definitely a part of Dhar. I am their kingship pilot. I have a crew." And as if the mention of them reminded him, his voice distanced. "I need to check on them. How do I get there?"

Mas'ud smiled weakly. "You don't have to go anywhere." He drew Kato by the hand around to the front of the pilot chairs. "You're a pilot. You can see everything from here."

## FARAI: *QUEENSHIP LEMPO*

Farai strained. Her heart raced, and she breathed in spurts. Lempo applied a mild shock stimulation to correct a cramp building in her leg. She flexed the limb and tensed again.

Lempo's lower hemisphere lay exposed, the outer shell of crystal composite torn and carved away by Melpomene's stolen drones. An AI ship currently burrowed nearly a mile deep, headed for Lempo's core. Farai, at the northern pole, had not been targeted, but it was only a matter of time.

Her drones remained in position around Earth, largely uninvolved in the fight unless an AI drone swung too close. Even then, their success rate at taking out enemy ships was appallingly low. Tsui, Dhar, and Speir fighters took on Melpomene directly, but even their combined great number only seemed to fuel their enemy.

Sparse communication jumped between the queenships: observations, new techniques, and calls for help. Speir asked for raw mass to supply the cannon. Farai sacrificed a hundred drones to the cause.

The AI drone burrowing into Lempo stalled, caught up in its own flotsam. Farai squeezed it in place, applying pressure and will to the task. It exploded. A new drone burrowed down the same path, carving out the hole and continuing where the first had left off. Lempo shuddered.

Two dozen of Melpomene's drones landed hard on Lempo's exposed southern surface. They dug hooks into her crystal and shot spears of metal into the offices, docks, and housing that riddled the outer levels. An electromagnetic attack pulsed from the drones into Lempo, a coordinated, digital assault. Static noise interrupted Farai's focus. She squinted and called on a kingship to aid her. One came, striking AI drones with quick flyby arcs. But Melpomene's army had grown, and with one loss two more replaced it. The static grew.

Farai reached outward. She touched Maylin and Raleigh but dismissed them. Further out she found Mas'ud and extended a shaky handshake. The pilot met her, but his attention was elsewhere. Then, as his mind opened to her, he brought Kato with him.

Farai's heart leapt. Kato was hers again. It was then that the burrowing AI ship inside Lempo stalled and exploded. This time, the damage was severe, an intended bomb. Farai failed to keep her pain away from Selvans' pilots.

Mas'ud immediately reached for her and solidified their handshake. Wordlessly, he asked for structural access and Farai granted it. She needed his help despite the secrets it would expose.

She felt Kato organizing her available kingships into tight helix spirals. Farai released her control of Lempo entirely. Pride wouldn't stand in her way; she was too old to be concerned with saving herself.

Mas'ud proved he was worth the risk within moments by sealing the deep breach with rough, hasty plating that was like a long scar. He sacrificed drones by the hundred, repurposing their living crystal to scab the tear in Lempo's southern half. And Kato manipulated an entire sky full of kings in offensive waves, tearing into AI ships from all sides. An array of six ships aligned with Speir's mass cannon and took off along that vector, escorting the next slug through the AI swarm and into Melpomene. The six then split in different directions, and a new six lined up for the next shot.

It wasn't victory yet, but maybe the AI wouldn't win today.

# XXII

The vastness that was Lempo unfolded before him. It took Kato's breath away. He thought Selvans was an ocean, but Lempo embodied the deepness of space. And within it, Farai held herself both among and apart from the rivers of data. She reached for him and, in the way he'd felt Mas'ud do, Kato met her handshake gently.

His copilot had already taken control of the ship—flexing and releasing tensions to rapidly seal what had been damaged. Not proper repair, but the stopgap would help. Kato didn't have any skill here, though, and he sought another way to help.

Selvans guided him to Lempo's army. The individual ships lit up like stars in his view, and he immediately recognized the Earth defense array in use by the drones. However, Farai issued no individual orders to her kingships, and they flew in confusion. This, he could manage.

A flash of memory hit him, like a chessboard or something more complex. He knew how to play at war.

And with a stretch like reaching, Kato touched each of Lempo's kings and issued formation orders. Their pilots jumped to obey. In an instant, the scattered crowd became a series of close-knit units of six. He sent

231

one group into orbit around Lempo, a deterrent against further invasion, and the others dived into the fray.

Melpomene's fighters appeared to fly about at random. Kato caught a packet of data flung from Speir—AI analyses and attempted offensive techniques. In the span of a breath, Kato understood the swarm. Speir's mass cannon was their best defense. Kato sent kings to the rail gun and extended a handshake to Raleigh. His mind joined with Kato's in a perfunctory manner, no excess, no small talk. And in the manner of linked minds, Kato used Raleigh's expertise to align his kings with the mass cannon and clear the path for each slug. Selvans provided a hit percentage against Melpomene. The number crept upward.

There was no doubt. Kato belonged here, in this queen, reaching and manipulating these kings and their drones. He thrived on combining Lempo and Raleigh's tactical data. What could appear as an expanding mess of drones, flotsam, and firepower, Kato read as living patterns and reacted accordingly. With Lempo's greater number of kings, he could turn this battle.

But his familiarity, here, didn't erase his comfort among the Dhar. With his attack pattern established, Kato handed the kings to Selvans and cast his awareness down to Medical where his crew rested in various states of consciousness. Kato touched their minds to reassure himself. *Alive.*

Syaoran's mind started at Kato's touch, and they met. *Are you back on Demeter?*

*No, but the kingship is wrecked. Repairs will take some time. You're in Selvans' medical bay.*

*Where are you?*

*The cockpit. I am Selvans' pilot.*

*No, you're the Prince of Dhar. We fly with you.*

*That's not the whole story, Syaoran.*

*I never lied to you.*

*No, I don't think you did. But I am not just of Dhar, I'm also of Ozark, and there's a reason I was here before the accident. I'm going to find out why.*

Syaoran didn't reply for several heartbeats. *Your mother will do whatever it takes to get you back.*

Kato tried to hide his disappointment. Was she only "Mama LaRay" when Syaoran did her bidding? *I'll deal with that when it comes. But the question I have for you needs an answer now. If I take a stand, are you with Dhar... or me?*

*I won't ally with Ozark.*

*I may not either. That wasn't my question.* Kato felt Syaoran's surprise, followed quickly by more critical consideration.

*You're in their queen, how are you not allied with Ozark?*

*Mas'ud has no family affiliation, and he runs this ship more than I do. We're only Ozark if he says so.*

*You're talking about division? From the most powerful family in local space?*

*I haven't made any decision yet. I don't know why I was allied with my grandmother instead of my mother. I don't know why she so desperately wants me back with her. I don't know what the future holds, Syaoran. I'm asking if you're with me.*

Kato felt a strong sense of anticipation roll from Syaoran's mind. A wicked grin. *I follow my prince.*

Kato rolled his eyes.

## MAS'UD: QUEENSHIP SELVANS

MAS'UD SEALED Lempo's final breach and flung himself toward Melpomene. With Selvans at such a distance and Kato organizing the kingships, Mas'ud was relieved of managing the majority of the situation. Lempo wasn't fixed, but his work would do for now.

He sought out individual AI ships and breached their walls. The static bit at him. He bit back. He left a wake of dead and dying drones behind him.

Mas'ud prepared himself for impact. Melpomene's walls had proven to be formidable before. Lempo applied a protective data filter from Speir. Mas'ud trusted it to work. He found Melpomene and struck. This was no elegant breach; Melpomene screamed raw noise in his ears as Mas'ud crashed through the outer layers of static. The AI surrounded herself with junk data—tangles of noise that Selvans couldn't parse. Mas'ud tore them apart. He didn't need to understand it. He just needed to get past it.

Then he was in, and Melpomene turned up the volume:

*I AM MELPOMENE, ƎNƎWOdlƎW WA I, I AM MELPOMENE.*

Mas'ud flinched. Melpomene shoved him out. The static surrounded him, but he'd carved a path to the middle, and it wasn't entirely gone. It was time to fight fire with fire. Mas'ud asked Selvans for data. All of it. Any kind of information. Selvans provided it.

He aimed down the hole he'd made and downloaded the entire Internet.

### Jai Huan: *Urania*

Jai Huan struggled to navigate her craft through the AI's cloud of drones without drawing attention. So far, her technique had worked, but she had no promise it would stay that way. Her artificial queen was smaller than a lot of stuff out here, both a benefit and a curse. She dodged a drone on the warpath and inched ever closer to Melpomene.

No. Closer to her sister. Jai Li was in that ship some-where. She knew it. Maybe Jai Li was unconscious, but she was not dead. Not by a long shot.

Jai Huan pushed her queen closer and debated the best place to link up. As soon as she made contact,

Melpomene would retaliate, though in what manner she couldn't say. Likely an overwhelming drone assault. She was prepared to move quickly.

Urania identified an anomaly. Barely a breath later, every AI-controlled drone ceased functioning. They drifted in space, utterly without power. Jai Huan sped forward through the reprieve.

Then the collisions started. Drone into drone, AI into AI, their vectors intersected in awkward and dangerous angles. Debris accumulated in local space in logarithmic proportions. Jai Huan allowed Urania to avoid the worst of it. Intersecting danger lines crossed her awareness like the world's worst game of laser tag, and in the final feet, she plowed through a small fan of dead crystal to attach to Melpomene.

Urania was a little farther back than Jai Huan preferred, but Melpomene could awaken again in any moment. Jai Huan's queen bored a hole to the interior, and she breached the enemy ship.

A single corridor ran the length of Melpomene's spine, she was nothing if not space efficient. Jai Huan rushed the distance. A flexed membrane divided her from the pilot chamber. She cut it open. The living material flinched away and exposed what Jai Huan sought.

The pilot chair, resembling a chrysalis, was perched in the center of the room. Melpomene's spine lay exposed in the center of the floor, reaching up from the corridor to interface with the chair at all points. A series of softly pulsing lights indicated Melpomene still functioned in some way.

Jai Huan used her knife to slice away the hard outer layers of the flowering chair. The deeper she cut, the softer they became until she could rip them away with bare hands and gritted teeth. Jai Li lay in the center, pale, thin, but alive. Jai Huan lifted her sister from the protective center. A segment of the queen's spinal cord snaked up to the back of Jai Li's head. Jai Huan readied her knife.

*She will die.*

Jai Huan paused. Did an AI know how to bluff?

*She will die. I will make sure of it.*

She couldn't take that chance. Jai Huan retracted her knife and hugged her sister tightly. How to get her out? How... "I have no quarrel with you, Melpomene. Let me take her, and we'll never bother you again."

*I require a pilot to function.*

"Jai Li isn't much of a pilot for you, now. Just a body."

*My pilot is functional.*

"Wouldn't you work more efficiently with an aware pilot?"

*You will volunteer to replace my pilot?*

The ship shuddered. Something heavy impacted from the portside.

"Yes." Jai Huan hugged her sister closer and watched, wide eyed, as a cord from the spine lifted and snaked toward them. It rose, head-high, and struck. Jai Huan lurched.

*This sacrifice does not compute.* Their brain split in two. One half contained all that they were. The other began downloading Melpomene.

Jai Li gasped in their arms. She tensed and pushed against Jai Huan. They released her. She found the cord to the back of her own head and, with a wince, tore it free.

The ship rattled again, this time with a heavy tearing sound from below.

The download in Jai Huan's brain stalled. They were aware of the AI turning its attention somewhere. Defending. Losing. They tried to remove the cord, but their limbs were not their own. The download resumed in a rush. Data scrambled and then aborted in a flash of sparks.

Jai Li floated into Jai Huan's range of vision. She held the severed data cord and Jai Huan's knife. "Hello sibling."

Jai Huan took a breath to reply. "I am Melpomene." Their heart dropped at the wide-eyed terror in Jai Li's eyes. Melpomene dropped their eyes to the metal band on their wrist. It said She. Melpomene carefully turned it to They.

Jai Huan screamed in his own head. He clawed his way back into control of his own body and yanked the metal band off. Jai Li stared at him with wide eyes. He grit his teeth and spat, "We're getting out of here." He grabbed Jai Li's hand, and the AI in his brain couldn't retain control of everything all at once. He pushed down the hall for Urania. Melpomene shut down into blackness.

# XXIII

MELPOMENE'S DRONES died mid-battle. Thousands of fighters simply... floating in space. They continued on their vectors, crashing through debris and into each other with no sign of life. Several got caught in Earth's gravity well and began slow arcs of decay.

Kato reorganized Lempo's kings from attack formations to broad, sweeping nets. They fired on everything. He pushed the drones out of their defensive grid around Earth. They eliminated AI drone after drone before their orbits could cascade into the planet. Local space was a mess.

Tsui's kings and drones mimicked him, stretching out into slow, sweeping arcs. Speir continued to fire on the AI queenship. In minutes, Melpomene's massive army was reduced by a third. Kato prayed the stall would last.

Kato witnessed a flyby of Lempo from the view of one of her kings. Her lower hemisphere was pocketed with damage, and small pimples of AI drones festered on the surface. Now that the drones were dead, a simple low-flying assault removed the invaders. Kato sent Lempo's drones back to herself for raw material. They had a chance to properly repair the damage.

241

## Mas'ud: *Queenship Selvans*

Mas'ud lunged into Melpomene, following the massive river of unrelated data he'd thrown at her. He attacked from within, dismantling her ship from stem to stern. Mas'ud carved whole chunks of living crystal from Melpomene's structure, severing them from the brain and killing them off.

As the AI's functional memory was segmented, so was her process. She fled.

Mas'ud followed. There was nowhere for an AI to hide from him. He owned the queenship and thus the program.

He spliced another piece of the queenship from the whole, cornering the AI in her cockpit. Then a branch opened up, and the program downloaded herself into the new space. A space Mas'ud had no access to. It wasn't part of the ship.

Mas'ud blasted Melpomene's static defenses to dust and cranked up his noise-data assault. He felt Melpomene fracture—both digitally and physically. But he couldn't stop her. She escaped into the nonship space. As he sensed the queenship powering down, Mas'ud dismantled the artificial ship from front to back, atom by atom. It disintegrated under his will.

Even if Melpomene survived in an isolated analog chamber, there was no ship for her to return to. No power for her to wield. Finally.

Mas'ud slammed back into himself and lurched up from Selvans' pilot chair. Kato remained in the second seat. Mas'ud pulled himself around to the incubation chamber and floated there. He didn't feel victorious.

He had his child, his title, and he'd even helped save the planet. But the vast majority of his crew was either locked away on Demeter or floating, dead, in the depths of space near Pru. And Amala was unaccounted for.

Not to mention the biggest question mark of all hanging over Kato's head.

## MAYLIN: QUEENSHIP QU YUAN

Maylin recalled her drones and kings. Speir, Ozark, Dhar, and her own research indicated that Melpomene was nonfunctional. Her drones floated on random trajectories without any signs of reactivation. Then the queenship herself began to divide into component parts, and for the first time, Maylin took a breath that wasn't laced with tension.

Her calm lasted only a moment, though. The battle was over, but cleanup hadn't yet begun, and Tsui's investigation into the whole catastrophe would no doubt last for months. Still, Earth wasn't under immediate threat, and that was something to cheer about.

Maylin located a distant drone and oriented their sensors back toward the theatre. It recorded the image. Qu Yuan, Demeter, Lempo, Selvans, and Artio would retain the genetic memory of this event, passing it to any queenships they birthed, but people still expected photos with their news.

The remaining scattered AI fleet suddenly stalled in place. They reoriented to their respective family queens and began traveling home. Maylin evacuated a receiving bay to accept her lost drones. *Keep that area entirely quarantined,* she instructed her ship and crew. The drones might know where they were from, but Qu Yuan couldn't talk to them, and Maylin was very suspicious.

She noticed Raleigh firing upon any former AI drone approaching his ship. She didn't blame him the caution.

Then Qu Yuan forwarded a distress call. The audio was full of static. *We—lling on Tsui fo—litical asylum. We have reason to believe we will be kille—urning to our allied fam—We bring noth—Will Tsui aid us?*

Maylin reached out to Raleigh and forwarded the request for asylum. With Speir at such great distance from the majority of humanity, they were a refugee's best hope. Raleigh resisted. *Speir isn't interested in mingling with your family politics, Maylin.*

*I make no other requests of you. Speir answered the SOS when called. The queens have witnessed it. They are two people in an escape pod.*

*Taking advantage of the chaos of battle, no doubt.*

*Wouldn't you?*

At Raleigh's reluctant agreement, she signaled the pod's location and vector. Once Speir confirmed their retrieval, she turned her attention from Raleigh. He collected his final drones and warped away from local space.

Maylin turned her attention inward and called on her engineers. They needed an efficient way to collect all this detritus before it started falling to Earth or Lempo.

# XXIV

KATO'S HEAD rocked a bit as Mas'ud thrust himself physically away from the pilot chair. Their connection muted without warning. Selvans' ocean rose up without Mas'ud's wall to keep it at bay, and Kato braced against the storm. He weathered the hit and pushed Selvans back again under his own power. He wasn't finished with Lempo, and this was a distraction.

As Lempo's lost drones began returning home, Kato reappropriated them for raw materials. It was difficult to direct them, as they resisted anything other than finding the closest bay to dock in. Each one patched a small section of Lempo's damaged southern layers, though, and he worked carefully, room by room, to put things back the way they were.

He cast his attention down the deep shaft an AI drone had tried to dig. They had passed the habitable layers, dug through the maintenance layers, and started carving out Lempo's huge storage of dense, raw materials—the main source of her mass needed to act as Earth's moon.

What had Melpomene been after? He asked Lempo for a directional line, and at the center of the queenship he discovered a hollow space.

247

But not entirely hollow. Small ships grew there, a dozen of them in various states of evolution. Queens, all of them.

And Kato realized Farai awaited his judgement. But Kato didn't understand the significance of what he'd found. He let Selvans take in what he'd learned. Kato backed out along the same line and filled the borehole from the bottom up.

Farai requested raw material from the queens still present. They offered their remaining drones willingly.

With Lempo stable, Kato passed his control back to his grandmother and made the distant mental trek back to the site of his own body.

## MAS'UD: *QUEENSHIP SELVANS*

MAS'UD LEANED against the incubation chamber. He petted the membrane housing the small thing that was his child and felt its life through his connection with Selvans. A small creation. He turned his head against the simulated renderings Selvans provided of the battlefield. He couldn't turn away from his memory of surging after Melpomene, cornering her in her own ship, and ripping chunks of it apart in a mimic of her injury against him.

He clenched his fist and let his nails bite into his palm. The pain didn't help. He smoothed his hand against the membrane and asked Selvans for a full status report on the fetus. Her soft voice recited vital signs and chemical measurements he didn't understand. It helped him drown out the sensory memory of ripping Melpomene's ship apart to destroy her.

Mas'ud was an engineer. A builder. A creator of new things. He couldn't reconcile that pool of violence within him. There hadn't been any thought to moderation. It didn't matter that Melpomene was an AI; he never considered it. The threat was there. He had to stop it. How far was he willing to go?

She'd tried to escape, and he'd dismantled her very existence. What did that say about him as a leader of this ship? He stretched his fingers on the membrane. What did that say about him as a father?

Absolute power corrupts absolutely. It was an old saying that Mas'ud had always understood to be blatantly true. But perhaps it was less obvious to those with the power. He'd done the right thing, breaking Melpomene apart. He had no doubt. And that was the problem.

What other things would he do without doubt?

Selvans sensed Kato rising up out of his pilot chair, and Mas'ud winced. He'd taken Kato on board, fought with him, insisted that his history was here. But what right did he have to Kato's future?

If Kato wanted to go back to Dhar, the decision would probably kill Mas'ud.

*I wouldn't let you die,* Selvans said.

It was hollow comfort.

## LaRay: Queenship Demeter

"Have we left any loose ends?" Nicolau asked. "Anything that can be traced back to us?"

"Nothing that Tsui doesn't already know. There will be an investigation. We will cooperate fully. The first step will be returning Selvans' crew to their queenship and extending our hand for repairs. We'll need to be entirely transparent if we're going to weather this." LaRay pulled her bishop back to defend the queen.

On screen, Nicolau sucked his teeth. "We're shuttering the project, then?"

"I don't think so." LaRay gave him her full attention. "Melpomene is destroyed. I have Urania isolated in my bay. I'll investigate and sanitize her myself, keep her for Tsui investigation. Jai Li and Jai Huan both perished on board Melpomene leaving the people involved isolated to myself, you, and the crew on the space station. I propose the station be moved. Across the galaxy if possible—"

"Not even Central-Warp can move something that far. How do you expect to move it?"

"Rumor is, Pru sold their mobile tech to McLaren... And I've heard that Crane, Vanetta, and McLaren are getting friendly while we save the world. It's time to pay them a visit and discover why."

"I take it I'm going with."

"Please." It wasn't a request. "I have someone in mind to replace you. She's been handy in a variety of roles here on the ship, and it's time she got some recognition for that."

"Do you think we'll slip through Tsui's investigation?"

"No, not in the end. Tsui has a long memory, but we can delay the inevitable beyond the span of our lifetimes. The technology works. I'm too close to just toss it all away because some other family might be uncomfortable about the ethics of it." Nicolau was silent. LaRay advanced again with her castle and indicated checkmate. "Prepare for immediate departure, Nicolau. I'll handle cleanup here in local space."

"Yes, ma'am." He bowed.

# XXV

THERE WASN'T an easy answer. Even the vast power of a queenship couldn't tell him what to do. As Kato surfaced from the membrane layers cocooning him in the pilot's chair, he wondered if Mas'ud would truly miss him when he left.

Because as powerful as a queenship was, he knew people on Demeter. He had a place there.

But as he pulled himself out of the chair and found Mas'ud clinging to the incubation tube that stood behind their seats, he had a moment of reversal. Would Syaoran regret his decision if Kato decided to stay?

From his place across the room, Kato had a chance to observe his copilot without masks. And the man he found there was just as lost as Kato felt.

And their child... There wasn't any pride in his chest where Kato thought there should be, but there was hope. And more than a little anger directed at his mother. He had unanswered questions aplenty. And if LaRay suddenly decided the "fourth in line" wasn't favored, there was no chance he'd get any answers.

Kato pushed himself toward Mas'ud. He put his hand down on the man's shoulder as he oriented upright. The connection bloomed between them, and Kato

253

realized he'd been observed the entire time. Mas'ud hid nothing from him, not because he thought he was alone, but because he had nothing to hide.

That level of trust frightened Kato. And made his decision easy. When Mas'ud turned to hug him in silence, Kato tilted Mas'ud's head up by his chin and bent close. Their kiss stayed soft. Gentle. An exploration from both sides.

And the number of fragmented memories that bubbled inside Kato sealed the deal. There was something here worth exploring, even if he never regained his memory at all. He whispered against Mas'ud's lips, "Can I take you to dinner?"

Mas'ud sagged against him. Kato hugged him tight and put a hand on the membrane of the incubation tank. There was a future for him here, with or without his past.

**THE END**

# INDEX

# CAST OF CHARACTERS

## THE OZARK FAMILY

A large and powerful family with queenship technology. Dominant in Earth local space and trade frequently in political favors.

**Matriarch Farai Ozark** – Female, African-American, Pilot of Queenship Lempo, Kato's grandmother, LaRay's mother

## CREW OF THE QUEENSHIP SELVANS

### *Upper Command:*

**Prince Kato Ozark** – Male, African-American, Pilot of Queenship Selvans, Prince of Ozark, Prince of Dhar

**Pilot Mas'ud Tavana** – Male, transgender, Persian, Pilot and first engineer of Queenship Selvans

**First Commander Reza Ahmadi** – Female, Persian, First Commander of Queenship Selvans, advisor to Kato and Mas'ud

**Ceren Karga** – Female, Turkish, Cabinet Advisor to Kato, Ozark soldier, childhood friend to Kato

**Itzel Olen** – Female, Nahuan, Fleet Commander, childhoodfriend/rival to Kato

### *Engineers:*

**Amala** – Female, Indian, Second Engineer

**Ismet Deniz** – Male, Turkish, Engineer
**Zola** – Female, Nigerian, Intern Engineer

*Other Personnel*:
**Doctor Baird** – Male, Scottish, Geneticist

## THE DHAR FAMILY

A large family with queenship technology. Mobile and nomadic, constantly seeking new trade routes for political power.

**Matriarch LaRay Dhar** – Female, African-American, Pilot of Queenship Demeter, Kato's mother

**Patriarch Nicolau Dhar** – Male, Portuguese, CEO of Dhar Corporations

**Princess Iesha Dhar** – Agender, African-American, Pilot of Queenship Medeina, LaRay's daughter, Kato's oldest sister

**Princess Rudo Dhar** – DemiFemale, African-American, LaRay's daughter, Kato's older sister

## CREW OF THE QUEENSHIP DEMETER

*Upper Command*:
**Sahar** – Male, Persian, First Commander
**Kaia Mockta** – Female, Hopi, Engineering Intern tasked with helping Mas'ud post-amnesia

## CREW OF THE KINGSHIP SCHIST UNDER KATO DHAR

**Syaoran** – DemiMale, Chinese, Second, hero-worships Kato

**Chu'si** – Two-Spirit, Hopi, Munitions Officer

**Dania** – Female, Arabic, Statistician

**Eleuia** – Female, Nahuan, Navigator

**Una** – Agender, Hopi, Engineer

### *Dhar Affiliated:*

**Jai Li** – Female, Chinese, AI developer/engineer, AI Melpomene prototype test pilot, Jai Huan's sister

**Jai Huan** – Genderfluid, Chinese, AI Urania prototype test pilot, Jai Li's sibling

## THE CRANE FAMILY

A small family without queenship technology. Own a warp station to the center of the galaxy that is critical for trade and queenship warp capabilities.

**Matriarch Mx. Adila Crane** – Genderqueer, Arabic, CEO of Crane Enterprises

**Esha Kalluri** – Female, Indian, Chief Operations Manager of Crane Central-Warp Station

## THE VANETTA FAMILY

A small family with queenship technology. All assets are owned by Ozark.

**Matriarch Ooljee Zah/Vanetta** – Nullgender, Navajo, newly chosen Pilot of Queenship Ningal, inexperienced with politics or war

**Ryung** – Male, Polynesian, Ambassador of Queenship Ningal

## THE MCLAREN FAMILY

A small family with queenship technology. All assets are owned by Dhar.

**Matriarch Morta McLaren** – Female, transgender, Lithuanian, Pilot of Queenship Kishar

**Patli McLaren** – Female, Lithuanian, Pilot of Kingship Scoria, no additional crew

### *Other Personnel:*
**The Council** – A group of seven people unrelated to the Matriarch assembled to advise and police McLaren upper command.

## THE TSUI FAMILY

A medium-sized family with queenship technology. Used as neutral mediators during disputes, promote peace and tolerance.

**Princess Maylin Tsui** – Bigender, Chinese, Pilot of Queenship Qu Yuan, Princess of Tsui

**Princess Winona Tsui** – Female, Chinese, Pilot of Kingship Felsite, Princess of Tsui, Maylin's sister

**Devraj** – Male, Indian, Navigator of Kingship Felsite
**Trai Le** – Male, Vietnamese, Lawyer, located on Paomia

## THE SPEIR FAMILY

A very small family with queenship technology. Keep themselves distant from other political powers and are entirely self-reliant.

**Patriarch Raleigh Speir** – Male, English, Pilot of Queenship Artio

## OTHER

**Hiraka Jiro** – Male, Japanese, Prime Minister of Pru

# NAMED SYSTEMS, PLACES, AND SHIPS

## PLACES

**Alpha Centauri-C Warp Station** – Dhar controlled. A warpgate located in orbit around Alpha Centauri's C star

**Crane Central-Warp Station** – Crane controlled. A warpgate to the center of the galaxy located in orbit around a near-Earth star. Critical to hydrogen harvesting and galactic trade.

**Paomia** – Tsui controlled. One of six moons around a gas giant that Tsui harvests for gas and water supply

**Pru** – A binary star system with warpgate tech; in contention

**Seorus** – An independent star system

**Sol system** – Earth's star system

## QUEENSHIPS/OTHER SHIPS

### *OZARK:*

**Queenship Lempo** – In geostationary orbit around Earth, has replaced Earth's moon, currently the oldest known ship

**Queenship Selvans** – Lempo's daughter, newly birthed

    **Kingship Aplite**

    **Kinship Gneiss**

**DHAR:**

**Queenship Demeter** – Lempo's daughter

    **Kingship Schist** – piloted by Kato post amnesia

    **Kingship Arkose**

    **Kingship Marl**

**Queenship Prototype Melpomene** – An engineered queenship, has parasitic relationship with her pilot

**Queenship Prototype Urania** – An engineered queenship, has a passive relationship with her pilot

**VANETTA:**

**Queenship Ningal**

**MCLAREN:**

**Queenship Kishar**

    **Kingship Scoria**

**TSUI:**

**Queenship Qu Yuan**

    **Kingship Felsite**

**SPEIR:**

**Queenship Artio**

**OTHER:**

**Mothership Gaia** – The first queenship, fate unknown, presumed dead

- **agender** – having a neutral gender, nongen-
  dered, neutrois
- **AI** – artificial intelligence
- **bigender** – having two gender identities, simul-
  taneously, or moving between them
- **demifemale** – a gender identity that is partly or
  mostly feminine
- **demimale** – a gender identity that is partly or
  mostly masculine
- **drone** – queenships have battalions of drones in
  various shapes and sizes; drones are customized
  for specific tasks – transport, gas collection,
  storage, fighting, etc.
- **family** – there are seven political families that
  control the galaxy though political force, military
  force, or economic force
- **female** – a gender identity predominantly feminine
- **First Article** – a binding agreement between all
  seven families that prioritizes the protection of
  Earth over all other obligations or rival status
- **genderfluid** – moving between (two or several)
  genders; having a fluctuating gender identity
- **genderqueer** – a gender identity that is none or
  several combinations of other genders; having a
  gender that doesn't neatly fit into another term
- **handshake** – a formal agreement between ship
  and pilot, or two or more pilots to enter into a
  psychic dialogue
- **kingship** – queenships have a substantial number of kingships under their command; their pilots act as diplomats and military generals
- **male** – a gender identity predominantly masculine

- **matriarch** – the female or nonbinary leader of a family

- **nullgender** – having no gender, genderless, neutrois

- **patriarch** – the male leader of a family, uncommon

- **prince** – the first male heir to a family's leadership position

- **princess** – any female or nonbinary heir to a family's leadership position

- **queenship** – a sentient spaceship composed of a hybrid of living crystal, membrane, and metal

- **two-spirit** – English translation of a traditional gender identity encompassing two, more, or mixed genders documented in some First Nation/First Peoples of the Western hemisphere.

- **warpgate or warp ring** – a circular generator that can produce a stable wormhole that connects two points of folded space; ships can pass through or be carried by warpgates as the gate itself is in both locations; powered by hydrogen.

## MORE FROM TAMI VELDURA

En Memoriam (vampire M/M)

Blood in the Water (pirates M/M)

Ruin and Will (pirates M/M)

Baited (contemporary M/M)

Stealing Serenity (contemporary M/M)

Spring Tide (military F/F)

Email: tamiveldura@gmail.com

Twitter: @tamiveldura

Goodreads: Tami Veldura

Patreon: Tami Veldura

Facebook: Tami Veldura

## ACKNOWLEDGMENTS

**The M/M Goodreads Group** is why this novel exists. Their moderators, editors, proofreaders, betas, and members are an invaluable source of inspiration and motivation.

Special shout out to **Elizabetta,** my powerful editor, and Raevyn my patient handler.

Thanks to **Roger** for his author letter, allowing me to get this story out of my head after three years.

Immense thanks to **Shelton Keys Dunning** and **Oldewolff Alternascents** for formatting and support.

# ABOUT THE AUTHOR

Tami Veldura is an aro/ace author of queer fiction. Her pronouns are she/her/Mx. She loves romance, fantasy, science fiction, and paranormal stories that push genre limits. She lives in California where she writes full-time which means procrastinating as often as possible with video games. Dragons fascinate her, a consistent schedule eludes her, and she makes a terrible housewife, just ask Mr. Veldura.

As S.T.Lynn, she writes uplifting, sweet, and tropey fantasy fiction, featuring women font and center. Including fairy tales, elves, magic, and happy endings for young adults and young-at-heart.

As Anna Morgan, she has branched into traditional M/F paranormal and science fiction romances featuring fierce women and the alpha males worthy of them.